An

this is one of my favorites!

FALLING FOR THE BOSS

by

J. Sterling

xx

FALLING FOR THE BOSS

Edited by:

Jovana Shirley

Unforeseen Editing

www.unforeseenediting.com

Cover Design by:

Michelle Preast

www.Michelle-Preast.com

www.facebook.com/IndieBookCovers

Please visit the author's website
www.j-sterling.com
to find out where additional versions may be purchased.

ISBN-13: 978-1-945042-48-5

Thank you for purchasing this book.

I hope you enjoy my Fun for the Holidays collection!

Other Books by J. Sterling

Bitter Rivals—an enemies-to-lovers romance

Dear Heart, I Hate You

In Dreams—a new adult college romance

Chance Encounters—a coming-of-age story

THE GAME SERIES

The Perfect Game—Book One

The Game Changer—Book Two

The Sweetest Game—Book Three

The Other Game (Dean Carter)—Book Four

THE PLAYBOY SERIAL

Avoiding the Playboy—Episode #1

Resisting the Playboy—Episode #2

Wanting the Playboy—Episode #3

THE CELEBRITY SERIES

Seeing Stars—Madison & Walker

Breaking Stars—Paige & Tatum

Losing Stars—Quinn & Ryson

THE FISHER BROTHERS SERIES

No Bad Days—a new adult, second-chance romance

Guy Hater—an emotional love story

Adios Pantalones—a single-mom romance

Happy Ending

THE BOYS OF BASEBALL

(THE NEXT GENERATION OF FULLTON STATE BASEBALL PLAYERS):

The Ninth Inning—Cole Anders

Behind the Plate—Chance Carter

Safe at First—Mac Davies

FUN FOR THE HOLIDAYS

(A COLLECTION OF STAND-ALONE NOVELS WITH HOLIDAY-BASED THEMES)

Kissing My Coworker

Dumped for Valentine's

My Week with the Prince

Spring's Second Chance

Summer Lovin'

Falling for the Boss

ULTIMATUM

JOSEPH

"I'M TIRED OF the cold," my mother said as she looked out my office window on the thirty-second floor.

Without even glancing up from my desk, I knew she was staring at the snow-covered park across the street. New York had been ravaged by storms lately. A cold front unlike any other in past years blanketed our city with thick white snow. It was beautiful to look at, but it sucked to live in.

My mom sounded almost bored, as if the city disinterested her somehow. To be fair, she probably was. I'd heard this particular sentiment many times over the years from her, but for some reason, it felt a little different today.

"You always say that." I finally looked up and waited

for her to face me and make her point. I knew that she had one. I could sense it coming. My mother didn't make unnecessary statements.

She turned, as if on cue, her weathered blue eyes meeting mine, even with the Botox. "I do, don't I?" Her lips curled up into a small smile and her face wrinkled with it.

"It's almost winter, Mom. We're always tired of the cold. And then we're tired of the heat in the summer. We're New Yorkers; we're not supposed to be happy."

My mother laughed as she nodded in agreement. "Fair point."

I waved my hand toward one of the couches in my massive corner office. "Sit down. Tell me what's really going on."

"Am I that obvious?" she asked before following my direction without arguing and taking a seat, her legs crossing at the ankles.

I stayed in the chair behind my desk and closed my laptop, so I could see her fully, giving her my devoted attention.

Ever since my father had been killed on 9/11, it'd been

me and my mom against the world. Losing him had been awful and ugly, and we were painfully reminded of it each year on its anniversary. Thankfully, it didn't hurt quite as bad as it once had, but the memory still seared like a red-hot poker at times. I couldn't watch any documentaries on what had happened that day without breaking down into hysterics. And TV shows or movies where buildings fell to the ground caused me to have mini panic attacks, where I fought to catch my breath.

It's not pretty, and it would be embarrassing if I gave a fuck. Which I don't.

That day had been mass chaos and panic, and if you hadn't been in the actual city, you had no idea what it'd felt like to be here. Pictures and television screens were one thing, but nothing compared to seeing it with your own two eyes, being worried with your own heart, and smelling the air that I could never accurately describe.

MY DAD HAD had a meeting with some finance guy at nine a.m.

"On time is late," he used to say, and I always naively

agreed. That was, until getting there twenty minutes early had literally been the death of him. If he'd been on time, he would have survived. But no, he'd had to be early and stepped off the elevator on the one hundred first floor of the North Tower five minutes before it got hit by a fucking airplane.

I heard the horrific sounds from my classroom that morning, but I had no idea what it was until all hell broke loose. All of our teachers were hysterical, and even Principal Rogers couldn't stop crying in the assembly room, where we'd all been forced to gather and wait. Principal Rogers never showed any kind of emotion, except anger. That was when I knew it was really bad. None of us could check anything though. Cell phones had stopped working; the networks were overloaded.

"Both towers were hit with planes this morning," Principal Rogers informed us, and my twelve-year-old brain played it off like it wasn't a big deal at first.

An accident, *I thought to myself.* Why is everyone freaking out? The Twin Towers are massive. They'll be fine. It's not like they can fall. We all know they were built to stand.

Another round of noise I couldn't begin to describe engulfed us, and the ground started to shake. We all frantically looked around at each other, but no one said a word. It was eerily quiet. A room filled with teenagers, not one of us making a sound. Principal Rogers excused himself and returned quickly, his face pale, his hands shaking.

"One of the towers just fell," he announced.

The assembly room exploded with cries and shouts. We all talked over one another, our utter shock apparent. Many of my classmates had parents who worked in the buildings.

When my mom finally showed up to take me home, it was the first time I'd stepped outdoors since it'd happened. By then, both towers had fallen, and the sky was an unnatural shade of gray, thick with debris that hurt to breathe in. My eyes burned.

"Your father," Mom started to say, her hand squeezing mine way too tight as we walked across the street and toward the building where we lived.

I was too old to be holding my mother's hand, but I allowed it.

I stopped walking. "What about him? Where is he?"

She shrugged. "I don't know."

"What do you mean, you don't know?"

I pulled out my phone and tried to call him, but the networks were still fucked. When they did work, the calls went straight to voice mail, and we prayed that he was just somewhere and couldn't reach us. Roads were closed. Mass transportation had halted. It wasn't out of the question that he was simply out of reach and would walk through our front door at any moment.

But when he still hadn't shown up or reached out by evening, Mom and I made our way to where the towers had once stood, pictures of him in hand to put up just in case anyone had any information or had seen him. We weren't the only ones. Hundreds had the same idea as we did, taping photos of their loved ones to walls with phone numbers, desperate for information that no one could give them.

To this day, it was still the most surreal and horrific experience of my life.

We'd eventually learned that not a single person from the company my dad had been meeting with got out alive.

There was no way to exit the building after the plane hit. Every stairwell had either been destroyed or was filled with debris or packed with smoke.

Dad never came home.

And instead of falling apart, Mom stepped up. She ran our staffing business, overseeing the daily operations and making sure everything was in the same tip-top shape my dad had left it in. We both grieved in our own ways, but we weren't alone. The entire country mourned with us, especially in Manhattan. It was helpful at times, but it was also exhausting. We couldn't go anywhere anymore without someone asking if we were okay or without running into someone who was mourning a loss of their own, barely holding it together. We were forever bound to thousands of strangers by one horrible moment in time.

AFTER HIGH SCHOOL, I'd wanted to come straight here, to the company, but my mom had forced me to go to college, like she and my dad had always planned for. She didn't want to take away my youth when so much of it had been stolen already in grief.

I begrudgingly agreed with her but ended up dropping out after three years when I realized I was doing nothing but wasting time. My end goal had always been to run my father's company, and I hated waiting for what felt like no good reason, except to party and get laid. I didn't need to be in college to do either of those things. So, I left, came straight here, and learned more about my future than I ever could have by staying in school.

I spent the next four years working in every department in the company, learning the ins and outs from each division's standpoint. Creating relationships with the department heads as well as the employees was invaluable to me and paved the way for how I wanted to run things—with an open-door policy. My goal was to be the boss you could talk to, not the one you talked about behind their back. I wanted to be a problem solver, not part of the problem. It was the absolute best thing I ever could have done businesswise, and I'd been running Martin Staffing and Management for the last five years with my mother silently by my side. Her being here was more for show than anything else, and we both knew it, although neither one of us dared to say that little fact out loud.

"I'm tired, Joseph."

Worry instantly filled me. My dad had said those exact three words the night before he was killed, and I never realized how much of a trigger they were until this moment. I pushed back from my desk and walked across the room.

"Are you sick? Are you feeling okay?" I asked before sitting down on the couch next to her and taking her hand in mine.

"I'm fine." She pulled her hand away and patted my shoulder. "I only meant that I'm tired of being here and not doing anything else with my life."

I knew exactly what she meant. After my dad had died, it was like a part of her world had stopped turning, and all of the dreams they had shared seemed to evaporate, the way his presence did. At first, I knew it was because she was concerned about the company and all of our employees. She felt an obligation to make sure that no one lost their job and that all of our clients continued singing our praises and recommending us while remaining completely satisfied with our services. With ease, my mother oversaw every detail, caught each oversight, and handled the curveballs that clients threw at us. That became her full-time job until it was clear that she no longer needed to hold on with both hands; Martin Staffing and Management was going to be more than just fine with me at the helm. But by that point, I think my mom had forgotten that she once had dreams of her own. She'd lost her way during the detour my dad's death had caused, and she had yet to get back on her own road.

It was always part of the plan that I would take over and run the company, but we never intended on it being so soon. Life had taught me that it didn't follow a script, especially not the ones we tried to write for it. To be honest, I loved what I did, but I would like my mom to have more of a life.

"What are you saying exactly?" I needed to push her or else she'd never get to the point—at least not directly.

My mother would hem and haw, hinting at what she wanted to do but never fully giving in to it. She had mastered the ability to talk herself out of anything before it was even a true option.

"I want to travel. I want to see the world. Your father and I had so many plans for after—" Her voice broke, and she paused. "After he retired."

"I know. You guys used to talk about it all the time," I said almost wistfully even though I wanted to keep my emotions out of it. It was hard whenever he got brought up.

"We had a lot of plans."

"You can still do them, you know? And you should. You had a list once, remember?" I asked, talking about the bucket list of travel places that used to hang on our fridge underneath a *Take Risks* magnet. It'd disappeared one afternoon, and even though I'd noticed its absence immediately, I never asked about it. Until now.

"I still have it."

I straightened in my chair. "You do?"

"Of course. I just couldn't bear to look at it every day. It's in my dresser drawer in the bedroom."

For whatever reason, that little nugget of information filled me with relief. It made me happy to know that my mom hadn't thrown everything in the trash, the way she had donated all of my dad's things to charity before the dust settled. I had known it was hard for her to be surrounded by his memory, but it was hard for me to watch them all get handed out to strangers.

"I came here to tell you that I have plans to go away. I'm going to travel for the next year"—she smiled wistfully—"if not longer."

"A year?" I said through my disbelief.

"Or more," she added again for clarification.

My body tensed. I loved my mother, and while I enjoyed having my own space, the idea of not seeing her for a year or longer had me spiraling a bit. I had never, in my entire life, gone more than three days without seeing her.

"Yes. But I can't in good conscience leave if—" she started, but I cut her off.

I knew exactly what she was going to say. "I've been running the company for five years, Mom. I've got this. Nothing will happen to our legacy or our employees or our clients. I promise you that."

"Joseph, you think I'm actually worried about you running the company?" She sounded almost offended.

My breath caught in my throat. "If it's not that, then what are you worried about?" I stood up from the couch and made my way back over to my desk. I was more comfortable there, felt more in command.

"You. You're an amazing CEO. You've far exceeded my hopes for the company."

"But?"

"But ..." Her eyes narrowed—she was clearly irritated because I'd interrupted her twice already. "Life isn't just about work."

I stopped myself from growling out loud in frustration and annoyance. We'd had this conversation one too many times in the past, and I'd thought I'd stopped them from happening again. I was too busy for love and all the things that falling for a woman required.

Women needed the kind of time and attention I wasn't ready or willing to give. Take into account how hard it was for me to actually meet someone wife-worthy in the first place. Considering I was always here or at corporate functions, and you had the second problem. Plus, to be honest, I had no interest in relationships at this point in my life. That didn't mean that I didn't fuck. I did. But it was with women who knew we had no future and who had zero expectations from me. Kind of women versions of myself.

Dating, marriage, kids were all something I wanted

and saw for myself but further down the road.

My mother knew that, but it still didn't stop her from lecturing me. "You need a partner. You need a teammate. I don't want you to be alone forever. This company won't keep you warm at night. It won't listen to your fears, or grow old with you, or share meals, take care of you, or love you back."

"Mom, I know," I started, ready to argue, but she wasn't having it this time.

Her entire demeanor shifted, her back straightened, and her face grew uncomfortably stern.

"No, you don't know." Her tone made me feel like a little kid who had just gotten caught stealing the last cookie from the cookie jar after being warned ten times. "You need to want more from your life, and if you don't start taking it seriously, I'm going to intervene."

"Intervene? What the hell are you talking about, lady?"

My mother hated when I called her *lady*, and I snickered to myself as she clenched her hands together, feeling like I'd won somehow.

"You know that Social Month is almost here, right?"

"Yes," I answered in a bored tone because it was the

same thing every year.

Social Month was thirty obnoxious days filled with industry events, auctions, benefits, and parties. Anyone in the staffing business who wanted to host any type of event did it during this thirty-day period; otherwise, you didn't do it at all. It was absolute madness and sheer hell, and I fucking hated it, but it never seemed to slow down or end. No matter how many people complained about this period of time, it was those same exact people who booked the yearly events and insisted that you attend every one of them.

When it had been suggested a few years back that we extend Social Month to happen twice a year instead of just once, I'd almost faked a heart attack on the conference room table to emphasize that Martin Management would not be participating at all if that happened.

It stayed scheduled for one hellish month from then on.

"If you don't bring a date to the events, I'm going to bring one for you. And I do not mean any of those ladies you have on rotation who come to your house at night."

How the hell does she know about that?

"I have quite a few women in mind that I think you'd

actually like. I'm sure I can narrow it down, if need be."

If I had been drinking anything, it would have come flying out of my mouth with her ludicrous suggestion. "You what? You can't be serious?"

"Oh, but I am. I want you to find love. I want you to be happy."

"I am happy!" I shouted like a petulant child, but this was fucking ridiculous, and she had to know that. I wasn't some guy who needed to be set up on dates by his mommy. This was absolutely insane.

"I want you to be happy in more than just one aspect of your life. I want to travel the world and know that you're here, giving your heart away and making memories of your own outside of these office walls." She sounded legitimately sad, like I was disappointing her somehow by not settling down. "I don't think I can leave otherwise. I can't go away, knowing you'll keep spending all of your days and nights here."

She had to be joking. I glanced around the office to see if there were cameras set up, recording my reaction. When I didn't see anything out of the ordinary, I let out an annoyed breath.

"Let me get this straight. If I don't bring a date to the events, you'll provide one for me? Is that what you're saying?"

"That's what I'm saying."

I looked at her like she'd gone half-mad because what kind of mother did this shit to her only son?

"You know this is crazy, right?" I shoved out from behind my desk and walked right over to the dartboard on the wall. I pulled the darts out and started throwing them. Hard.

"You call it crazy; I call it creative," she countered as I continued throwing.

"I can find a different woman to bring to every event if I want, Mom. You know I don't do that."

My mom knew that I never brought dates to these things. It was one of my personal rules—no public appearances with someone I wasn't serious about. That person and the public always got the wrong idea.

She tsked me, her head shaking. "Not a different woman, Joseph. Just one. One girl for all the events you attend, or I will find one for you."

"The press is going to have a field day with this," I

mumbled under my breath.

They'd been hounding me for the last five years, printing questions and starting rumors about why I always showed up alone at Social Month events. They called me the Anti-Playboy, New York's Loneliest Bachelor, questioned whether or not I even liked women—*spoiler alert: I do*—Casanova's Other Brother, Bad Romeo, Clearly Not a Ladies' Man, the Un-Seducer, Not Don Juan, Second String, and my personal favorite, Not-So Prince Charming.

"Wonder what they'll call you now?" The sly grin covering her face made me want to punch a hole in the damn wall.

Was this some kind of joke to her? Messing with my personal life wasn't funny, not in the slightest. I wanted to be left alone … to work and close the deal I'd been working on for the better part of the last year. The last thing I needed was to show up at Social Month with the same woman on my arm and send the press into a frenzy. I absolutely did not have the time to handle that kind of crap while running a multimillion-dollar company I was trying to expand.

"You've lost your damn mind. You know that, right?" I cracked my knuckles, wondering how the hell this was an actual conversation I was having.

"Sometimes, the people we love need a little push." She extended her hand from the couch, and I walked over to her, reached for it, and helped her up. She stood tall and brushed out the invisible wrinkles in her skirt with her hands.

"This is more like a shove. With a long fall that's not going to end well," I breathed out, my heart racing in my chest.

"You never know; you might find true love." She pulled me in and squeezed me tight.

"The woman I'm already dating isn't going to like this," I lied through my teeth and wondered just where the hell that had come from.

My mom pulled away quickly and measured me with her eyes. "The what? Don't toy with my heart, Joseph."

I cleared my throat and took a step back from her. "I'm not. I've been dating someone for a little while now." I continued the lie for no good reason other than I couldn't seem to stop myself.

"Who is she?"

"You don't know her." I avoided making eye contact, peering past my mother's inquisitive gaze and straight at the wall.

"Well then, I look forward to meeting her." She patted my cheek before turning on her heel and walking out of my office.

UNBELIEVABLE

JOSEPH

INSTEAD OF FINDING something to throw against my wall, I shouted for my assistant, knowing she'd help me see reason and keep me calm. "Kaylaaaaaaaa!"

"I'm coming, jeez!" she yelled back as she hustled into my office, notebook in hand, and closed the door behind her. "Stop shouting like a crazy person. You'll scare people," she chastised me before asking, "Couch or desk?"

The question had become one of our routines even though I never responded with couch and she knew it.

"Desk," I bit out, annoyed.

All five foot two inches of her hurried to one of the two chairs opposite of mine and sat, tossing the notebook on top of the aged wood with a loud thud. "What is the matter with you? Why were you yelling?" she asked, and I continued wearing a hole in the floor instead of sitting. "Stop pacing and sit already," she demanded, and instead of glaring at her like I wanted, I begrudgingly moved to my chair.

Bossy Kayla had been hired as my assistant two years after I started as CEO. She was my eleventh hire. We were nearly the same age and had hit it off immediately even though I'd fought against interviewing her in the first place and almost had the whole thing called off. I had naively thought that hiring a woman close to my age was a bad idea, but every other *experienced* assistant before her hadn't worked out, and I found myself growing increasingly desperate.

Being the number one staffing company for high-level executives in New York City, you could imagine how ironic and infuriating it was to not be able to find myself someone worth a damn. I needed someone I felt comfortable with, who understood the way I thought about the business, who I could eventually trust implicitly, and who would make my daily life easier, not more complicated. Basically, I needed an assistant who wasn't hell-bent on screwing her boss—i.e., me.

The best part about Kayla was that she had zero interest in me romantically—trust me, I sensed those kinds of things. And it wasn't that she didn't find me attractive—I knew she did, but that was as far as her feelings for me went. It was the same for me. She was pretty, but I didn't want to sleep with her. I knew how vital she was to my daily operations, and I vowed to never do anything to screw that up.

Eventually, a genuine friendship had formed, and I'd found out later—much later—that she wasn't attracted to men at all. She'd started to feel like family after our first year working together, the little sister I never had who actually did what I told her and let me boss her around.

Sometimes.

I filled Kayla in on what my mom had just informed me, and she started to laugh hysterically. She sat in front of me, her hand over her stomach, laughing her tiny ass off.

"You think it's funny?"

"Little bit," she said through her laughter.

"Can you be serious for one second?" I demanded, and she tried to stop laughing, which only made her laugh harder. I folded my hands on top of my desk and waited while I glared at her.

"Stop looking at me like that, or I'll never be able to stop." She pointed at my face, and I started laughing too.

Kayla was the only person in the office who could get me to unwind and relax. I appreciated that fact more than I let on.

Once we both calmed down, I exhaled a long breath. "Can you believe she's doing that?"

"Actually, I can."

I knew my face did little to hide my shock. Of all people, I assumed Kayla would be on my side, see things my way, like she usually tended to, and realize just how insane this request was.

"You can?"

"You have no life outside this office, Joseph. She's your mother. She worries about you," she explained like everyone in the world knew this fact.

"There's something else," I said.

"What else could there possibly be?" Kayla shrugged at me, still smiling.

"I told her I was already dating someone."

I waited for Kayla to laugh at me again, but she only looked shocked instead, her mouth dropping open.

"Why would you do that?" She sounded exasperated and concerned because she knew that my problem was about to become her problem as well.

"I panicked!" I said, reaching for a pen and tossing it in the air before catching it.

"Wait." She pushed back from the chair and walked to my window, staring outside for three beats before turning to face me again. "Are you dating someone? You can't be, right? There's no way that I wouldn't know about it."

"No, I'm not," I clarified, and she sat back down in her chair.

"Okay, so who did you tell her you were dating?"

"I didn't specify. I just said it was someone she didn't know."

Kayla flung her hands together in prayer pose and leaned into them. "We can work with this. Just give me a second to think."

"How? It's not like I can tell my mom that you and I are dating."

"Ew, why would you tell her that we were dating?"

She threw her hands down and looked up at me, her expression almost disgusted. Any normal male would have been offended, but I was clearly not normal.

"I didn't tell her we were dating," I said again.

"Sorry. I didn't mean ew, like you're gross to look at or anything." She waved a hand toward my face. "It's just that …" She was flustered, and it was funny, actually watching her squirm for once. Kayla was always fairly composed and let things roll off her back. "I think of you like a brother, and she has to know I'm gay. Right?"

I ignored the last question because I honestly wasn't sure what my mother knew about Kayla's personal life. "I feel the same way, Kayla. Calm down."

She narrowed her eyes before doing as I asked and inhaling a long breath.

"How am I even supposed to meet someone? I'm always working. Most women don't like coming in second to a career. And the ones who don't mind it, I'm not interested in."

Kayla grinned. "You mean, you don't want a pretty little thing on your arm to parade around town and make all the other boys jealous?"

"A trophy wife?" I scoffed. "Definitely not."

Kayla stopped smiling and grew serious. "I know. I can't see you with someone like that."

I lifted my head and met her wide brown eyes straight on. "Who can you see me with?" I asked, wondering what kind of impression I gave off in her perspective.

She shrugged her shoulder. "I'm not sure," she said, but for some reason, I didn't quite believe her. Maybe it was the shit-eating grin that suddenly appeared on her face.

"I think that's part of the problem," I started to overexplain. "I've never really thought about it either."

"I'm aware. They don't call you the Not-So Prince Charming for nothing." Her eyes practically rolled right out of her head at the use of one of my trademarked nicknames.

"You know, I'll never understand why being single is such a bad thing. If I was bringing a different woman to every event during Social Month, they'd print a bunch of shit about what a womanizer I was. And not in a nice way."

"Yeah, but they'd secretly worship you for it too," she

added before I could keep talking.

"No shit. Why is that?"

"Because it makes you hard to tie down. Like, you've had *soooo* many women, so who will be the one to actually capture your heart? And what makes her so special?" She mimicked like she was conducting an interview. "We're a fairly messed up society when it comes to love and what we consider romantic."

I wished I could disagree with her, but it was true.

"For the record, I like that you don't bring random women to the events. Your penthouse is another story." She stuck out her tongue like the thought made her sick and she might puke all over my desk.

"And there's only two of them," I defended.

While I didn't have the time or desire for a real girlfriend, I still had needs and wanted good sex. The women on my speed dial did as well. They were both incredibly successful females who were looking for love about as much as I was. The relationship was mutually beneficial. No strings. No feelings. No public appearances. Fuck and leave.

"Would any of them do this for you?" Kayla asked.

I shook my head so hard that I thought it might fall off. "Not a chance. And somehow, my mother seems to know about them as well, so that's off the table."

Kayla slapped a hand on the desk with a loud pop. "I swear I did not tell your mom about those women. But back to the point." She started tapping her pen on top of her notebook. "I think your mom is serious about this, so we only have one real option."

Leaning forward, I placed my elbows on the desk and gave her my full attention. "I'm all ears."

"We have to find you someone and make your mom think you're happy, so she'll go on her *Eat Pray Love* trip."

She flipped open her book and started scribbling quickly as I tried to make sense of her words.

"What the hell is an *Eat Pray Love* trip?"

Kayla waved me off. "Never mind. It doesn't matter. Do you have any ex-girlfriends from college that we can pull from?"

"Pull from?" I had no idea what the hell Kayla was talking about. Sometimes, I swore that females had their own language that only they could understand.

She leveled me with a look that screamed for me to keep up. She snapped her fingers at me. "I'm trying to make a list. Girls from your past? Anyone we can ask to do this for you? Do you a solid? A favor? Do you get what I'm saying?" she asked like I was the dumbest male on the planet.

I shook my head. "My mom would never buy it being anyone from my past. She wouldn't believe it for a second. It has to be someone that she doesn't know."

Holy shit. What the hell am I doing? I can't believe that I am not only actually entertaining this idea, but contributing to it as well.

"This wouldn't be so hard if you actually wanted to fall in love," she chastised.

"You're one to talk," I chastised back.

For as much shit as Kayla gave me, I didn't see her prancing around with a serious girlfriend or a ring on her finger either.

"Hey! At least I try. I go on dates every week," she answered with a snarl, and I couldn't hide my shock. "And I think I might really like the girl I met last weekend."

"How the hell do you meet so many girls anyway,

Sanderson?"

Sometimes, I called Kayla by her last name. She always pretended to hate it, but I knew she loved it. I'd overheard her on the phone one time, telling someone that it made her feel like she was part of a team.

Groaning, she said, "It's called dating apps, genius. You should try one."

"Not gonna happen." I wasn't opposed to dating apps for other people, but there was something about them that didn't appeal to me. They were the very last thing I could ever see myself doing.

"Well, how did you find the women you sleep with now?" she asked.

I realized that I'd never really talked about this with Kayla before. While she knew far more about my life than anyone else, that always felt like crossing the line. I hesitated before she prodded.

"Just tell me. I know everything else about you."

I huffed out and said it all in rapid-fire before I could second-guess and stop myself. "One lives in my building, and the other one is an old business associate."

"How convenient." She sounded a little annoyed while

I sat there, surprised that she could even understand what I'd said in the first place. I chalked it up to another one of her female superpowers. "Well, for the rest of us, we have to use dating apps. Do you know how hard it is to meet someone?"

"No," I answered honestly because it was the truth. "Because I'm not trying to meet anyone, remember?"

"Ugh! See, you're not even open to the possibility of love. This is why your mom is never going to leave and live her life. Ever. She's going to sit here and babysit you until she dies. And you'll have no one to blame but yourself."

She was baiting me, pushing my buttons, hoping I'd snap. But my assistant knew me better than that.

"I'm not open to love *right now*." I emphasized the timing. "I'm still earning our clients' trust and trying to expand our company internationally. You know that. My mother knows that. I don't have time for a relationship. It wouldn't be fair to expect anyone to try to be with me right now."

My dad had built an empire with Martin Staffing and Management in New York, but it was my dream to take it abroad. The majority of our clients had multiple offices located across the globe, and it was a missed opportunity to only focus on their stateside ones. It'd become my goal to expand our company to Europe—London specifically—and I didn't have time for distractions. Not until I made this a reality.

"I know, but your mom needs to think that you're trying to have a life outside of this building."

"So, what do we do?" I acquiesced because I knew I had no choice.

"Let me go back to my desk and think about this for a second. You have a meeting in five minutes anyway. We'll reconvene after it ends," she said.

Before I could respond, she was out the door, and I was alone.

PAYING FOR DATES

JOSEPH

WHEN MY MEETING ended, Kayla popped back into my office, uninvited, and sat back down.

I glanced at her. "You thought of something?"

"Yeah. But you're not going to like it." She shook her head and made a face that told me I definitely wasn't going to like what she suggested.

"What is it?"

"There are some firms that specialize in this kind of thing." She said the words so quietly that my brain almost didn't pick up exactly what she was saying.

But when it clicked into place, I mentally took back my previous thought about dating apps and decided that *this* was the very last thing I would do to meet a woman.

"I know you're about to freak out, but just listen." She

put one hand in the air toward my face to get me to stop talking before I even started, but it didn't work.

"No. I can't do that. I can't go to some firm to find a date!"

"But it's not real. You'd just be paying her to be your fake date." She couldn't even get the words out without giggling.

"Are you going to stop laughing at me, or should I fire you?"

"Definitely fire me. But please give me a good severance package, so I can spend a month in Bali, doing nothing but working on my tan with a hot Balinese woman."

Short of Kayla betraying my company secrets and selling my soul to the devil, there was very little she could do that would get me to fire her, and she knew it.

"So, are we a go for the dating firm?" she asked, her expression serious as she put her pen in her mouth and bit down.

"That's the only thing you thought of this whole time?"

"Hey," she started to argue, but I interrupted.

"We just need to slow down a second," I said, my insides twisting.

"What's the hang-up?"

"It's kind of creepy, is it not?" I asked because it felt like it was.

She shifted in her seat before tossing her dark hair from her shoulders and onto her back. "It's not though. Listen. It's a business arrangement. You don't want to fall in love. These women aren't there for love. It's a win-win."

She pulled out her phone and started typing frantically on it. "Okay, these are the five high-profile firms for the rich and famous in the city." She winced as she said the words out loud, gauging my reaction before continuing her spiel. "Basically, they sound like high-class escort services, I guess?" She shrugged, clearly in as unfamiliar territory as I was.

"So, I'd pay some girl to be my fake girlfriend for Social Month, and my mom will be happy and go check off the things on her travel bucket list?"

Kayla's face pulled together. "List? I guess that sounds about right."

"And this woman wouldn't expect anything from me because I'd be paying her, right?"

"That's the gist of it, I think."

My brain spun a mile a minute. I had no idea what the right thing to do was, but I knew I couldn't really try to find a woman like my mom had suggested. I wasn't in the place for it. God, how had this become my life? An hour ago, the only woman even remotely on my radar had been the one I planned on fucking later. The one who would leave the second we were done and walk out of my apartment like nothing had happened.

"I'd be mortified if this got out to the press. Could you imagine the headline? 'The Anti-Playboy Turns into the Pays-for-It Punk'?"

She quickly stopped whatever she was doing on her phone. "No way would I let them meet with you before I vetted them first. I think the whole point of those firms is so that it doesn't get out. Obviously, the woman would sign a nondisclosure agreement, where she would be forbidden from discussing the details of your relationship or anything about you."

"There has to be another option," I said, shaking my

head and leaning back so far in my chair that I thought I might break it.

"There is. You could actually try to find a real woman on your own, or you could let your mom set you up, like I know she's dying to do. But then that poor girl would probably fall head over heels in love with you and want twenty of your little staffing babies."

The thought didn't excite me. It didn't cause my heart to race or my pulse to speed up. It gave me the exact opposite feeling actually—dread. It coursed through my veins, and I knew I wasn't ready for any of that.

Running my fingers through my hair in frustration, I responded, "I need a no-strings-attached type of deal."

"Then, we're going to have to call one of these places. It's our only hope. I wouldn't have even suggested it if I thought we had another option. I'll research them all first, meet with the owners, find out everything I need to before I let you work with them. Okay?" She tried to reassure me, but I was still hesitant.

"I trust you with all that," I said, and I meant it. I knew Kayla would never let me get into a situation that wasn't good for me. "I just don't like it. Why can't I just be free to focus all my time on work and worry about love and babies and shit later?"

"God, you remind me so much of Sutton that it's annoying," she said before her jaw slacked open. She quickly snapped it closed again, her lips pressing together tightly.

"Your psychotic roommate?" I asked, horrified.

After three years of working together, I knew way too much about Kayla's personal life, including her best friend and roommate, Sutton. She was the only person Kayla ever spoke about with consistency. To be honest, I only half-listened whenever Kayla went on a rant, talking about their excursions. I knew it was shitty of me, but as a guy, we only cared so much about people we didn't know or didn't plan on fucking. And Sutton's name was at the top of my DO NOT TOUCH list.

"She's not psychotic!" Kayla snapped back.

"I have memories that beg to differ." I leaned back in my chair and folded my arms across my chest.

I'd met Sutton once before, and it hadn't gone well. If my drunken haze remembered correctly, which was fuzzy at best, I'd called the woman a hot mess—or something like that. But in my defense, she had been holding a lighter toward my balls, threatening to light them on fire!

"You called her an evil troll," she yelled, and I started laughing 'cause that shit was funny.

"I'm sure she deserved it."

Kayla sucked in a loud, long, annoyed breath. "Shut up for one second and listen. Talking to you is like talking to the guy version of her. *Babies later. Why can't I work? Why does everyone want me to do something I'm not ready to do?*" She said the last few sentences in some silly, mocking tone.

"So?" I pushed, my tone, irritated, because even though Sutton was a redheaded stunner, she was clearly a fucking psychopath.

Why are redheads always the crazy ones?

"She doesn't want kids yet? Big deal. Is she running an empire I don't know about? Is she rich, insanely good-looking, and have a fetish for fast cars? Get called names in the press daily? Have men tried to land her for her money?"

Kayla's lips twisted like she'd bitten into rotten fruit. "Ew. Full of yourself much? And no to all of the above, by the way. I just meant how she has no interest in dating right now, just like you. She always talks about how no guy likes being second to her residency. Just like you. And only other doctors and medical personnel understand her way of life, but she doesn't want to date any of them because they're all egotistical assholes who think their shit doesn't stink," Kayla said with strength, like she was delivering the closing argument at a trial.

"Interesting." I smiled a little to myself, but I still wasn't convinced.

"Yeah. Now that I think about it, you two sort of have a lot in common." Kayla suddenly grew silent, her eyes looking past me and straight out the window. "How have I never put that together before now?" she practically whispered. "I know why. 'Cause you two hate each other," she continued talking to herself.

"What are you thinking, Sanderson?" I snapped my fingers once, bringing her focus back to me.

"Maybe we won't have to use one of those firms after all?" She dragged it out like a question, and I found myself more than a little curious.

"Let me see her picture again. A recent one." The last

time I'd seen the little wannabe fire starter, it was two years ago. A lot could happen to a person in two years.

Kayla pressed some buttons on her phone before turning it toward me. I reached for it and studied the face staring back at me. Long red hair, green eyes, and full lips.

"She's gorgeous." The words slipped from my mouth. I hadn't meant to say them out loud, but fuck it; it was the truth.

"Smart too," Kayla added, reaching for her phone, and I handed it back, hesitating slightly.

I wanted to text myself that photo so I could look at it later, study it more, or use the way those lips to jerk off to. The image of her holding a lighter toward my nether regions flashed in my mind, and I realized that no sane man jerked off to a chick who wanted to dismember his … well, member.

"Once again, I beg to differ. A lighter, Kayla. She had a lighter aimed at my balls," I explained.

"Yeah, yeah. I remember." She waved me off like this sort of thing could happen to anyone. "She never told me what you two were fighting about. Care to fill me in?"

Fighting? We'd been fighting? I barely knew the

woman.

"I have no idea. I was hammered that night, remember?"

She threw her head back slightly. "That's right." She snapped her fingers. "That was the double-shot bartender party."

Apparently, one of the bartenders had had some sort of grudge against a rival company of mine. He thought it would be funny to give all the executives and higher-ups double and triple shots of their orders without telling them. Almost everyone was off their rocker before dinner was even served. The only people who had been spared the humiliation were the ones who didn't drink.

"This might be our only option, Joseph. At least tell me you'll think about it."

"Is she taller than you? I can't run around with a sprite on my arm." I wasn't trying to be a dick, but my six-foot-four frame always looked silly in company pictures, standing next to Kayla.

"I'm not a sprite," she growled, her face looking like a cartoon character, and I couldn't stop laughing. "But she's a normal height, gargantuan."

"How tall is *normal* to people like you?" I teased, and her eyes pulled together.

"She's five-six."

That worked for me. But I still wasn't sure that I should be taking an evil troll to these events. "What if she does something crazy again?"

"She won't," Kayla pushed. "The next morning, she was mortified about how she'd acted and the things she'd said."

God, I wish I could remember any of that.

"I bet she was."

"Sutton doesn't normally act like that," Kayla added, and I shook my head, not sure what to believe. "You pushed her buttons."

"And neither one of us knows how I did it or what I apparently said?" I wasn't going to take the blame for something I wasn't sure I'd even done. And who the hell threatened a man's balls?

"Nope."

"Do you think she'll do it?"

"Not a chance," Kayla said, and my expression fell.

"Really?"

"No. She hates you."

"*She*"—I emphasized the word—"hates me?" I scoffed, jerking my head back and shaking my head like this whole thing was ridiculous. "Why would you even bring her up then?" I found myself getting even more annoyed … and competitive. I was not the type of man who lost easily, and now, this was something I needed to win. Even though it would probably be a huge mistake.

"The idea just slipped out. I hadn't planned it. But there's no way in hell she'd do something like this."

"Kayla," I growled, my jaw clenching.

Kayla looked away from my murderous eyes and up at the ceiling, as if the white tiles would provide her with some sort of wisdom. Apparently, it worked because within seconds, she said a single word with a sinister smile plastered across her face. "Money."

"Money?" I repeated, needing more details.

"Yeah. She has a ton of debt. Not that she won't get out of it, but I mean, it's going to hang over her head for the next twenty thousand years or so. You know, typical med school stuff."

I sat up straight, half-tempted to open my wallet and

throw wads of cash at her. "Well, that's easy. I have lots of money."

"Yeah, yeah." She waved a hand at me before pushing away from the desk and standing up. Not that you could really tell the difference between her sitting and standing. God, she really was short. "By the way, I want a raise if she agrees."

"Better get her to agree then," I said before adding, "And no lighters or matches are allowed in her possession."

What the hell am I doing?

NO EFFIN WAY

SUTTON

I TRUDGED THROUGH the front door of my apartment, my mind solely focused on the scalding hot shower I wanted to take. *Maybe I'll take a bath instead*, I thought for a second as my feet screamed at me to get off of them.

Twelve-hour shifts weren't easy, but they were totally worth it. Or at least, they would be once I was a burn specialist.

"Yay, you're home!" My roommate, Kayla, practically bounced down the hall to greet me. I never knew if she would be home or not—her work schedule was almost as demanding as mine. "You look like shit."

She pressed the back of her hand against my forehead, and I swatted it away.

"I don't have a fever. I'm not sick. I'm just tired."

"How tired?" she asked.

I shot her a look that told her I didn't have the energy for her kind of crazy tonight. Kayla could have me dressed up and drinking vodka tonics at some bar before I even knew how we'd gotten there.

She was always coming up with over-the-top ideas, and I usually went along with them. I mean, women really shouldn't go out alone, right, even if they were searching for other women? The city wasn't always safe, and I would never forgive myself if something bad happened to her because I'd sent her out to party alone.

"I could probably sleep standing up. That kind of tired," I said before asking, "Why?"

Kayla gave me an odd smile before pulling me toward our couch and sitting us both down.

Oh, that feels nice. I might never get back up again. I now live on this couch. Please forward my mail.

"Okay, before you freak out, just listen," she started off slowly, and I felt my entire body tense. No good conversation started with *before you freak out*.

I fidgeted but stayed seated. Partly because I was convinced my feet would give out on me the moment I tried to use them again and also because this was suddenly the most comfortable couch on the planet. Who cared that it was from my mom and so worn down that you could almost feel the support bar under your butt? Not me. At least, not right now.

"Okay, so," she tried to talk, but I interrupted.

"Kayla, don't drag whatever this is out. Just say it," I snapped but only because if she didn't spit it out soon, my eyes would close and not open again until morning.

"Joseph needs a date to the Social Month events, and I told him you'd do it." Her head whipped back as she braced for my response.

I suddenly felt anything but tired. "Joseph? As in your jerk-off of a boss, Joseph?" I stuttered his name because the one time I'd met the guy, I'd made a complete ass out of myself. Sure, he'd deserved it for saying the things he'd said to me and setting me off, but still. I was embarrassed and completely okay with going the rest of my life without ever seeing his stupidly smug face again. "And you told him I'd what?"

"Go with him to some of the events." She winced and shrugged a shoulder.

"He called me an evil troll, Kayla!" I shouted, and she started laughing. "An evil troll! And that was after insulting me numerous times."

"He's sorry," she said, and I narrowed my eyes at her.

"No, he's not."

"You're right. He's not." She exhaled loudly. "But I'm sure he will be. He can be. Whatever you need."

"I need him to go back in time and take away all the stupid shit that came out of his mouth so that night never happened the way it did."

"It can't be that bad. You never told me what he said to you anyway," she pushed, and I shook my head.

"It was bad. And I'm not repeating it," I growled.

The memory of Kayla's drunken boss being a complete asshole to me for no reason played in my head. I'd thought I'd gotten over it. The man meant nothing to me, but the way I was feeling right now, it could have happened last night—my anger felt so fresh.

"You're our only option," she announced, as if that made it a done deal.

"I can't be. There has to be someone else. Anyone else," I argued. "I don't have time to go on dates. Why would you do that? Why would you suggest me, of all people? We can't stand each other."

She threw her hands in the air before pulling at her short brown layers. "Because he needs a date or else his mom will never leave and *Eat Pray Love* her life away!"

It was my turn to pull hair, and I wrapped my red locks around my fingers. "What? Stop. Slow down. Start from the beginning, and I'll try to stay awake." I bit back a yawn. "You're not making any sense."

I listened as Kayla did her best to fill me in on what Joseph's mom had said to him. The only problem was … *I didn't care.* The issue seemed so mundane, so irrelevant to my life that I couldn't seem to muster up any emotion to actually give a shit.

"So, what do you think? Will you do it?" my roommate asked, her tone hopeful.

"No."

"No?" she repeated, sounding exasperated. "Why the hell not?"

Shaking my head, I was too tired to mince words, too exhausted to play nice, so I didn't. "Because I don't care, Kayla. Poor little rich boy's mommy won't go away and leave him alone to run his multi-million-dollar company? I don't have time for this kind of thing. It's stupid. And I'm not stupid."

"I already told him you'd do it."

She made it sound like I didn't have a choice in the matter, but this was my life, and I had nothing but choices.

"Well, that's on you then. I never said I would. And you knew damn well I wouldn't agree to this."

Her lips formed a snarl as she tossed her head back against the cushions. "Of course I knew you'd say no." She lifted her head to look me square in the eyes. "But that's why I asked him for some incentive."

What could she have figured I'd possibly want or need that would get me to agree to this potential shitshow?

"Let me guess," I started, knowing there was only one thing that motivated people to do things like this for others. "Money?"

Her eyes grew two sizes too big. "Lots of money, Sutton."

"I don't need his money." She knew that as much as I did.

Neither one of us was rolling in tons of cash, but we

survived. We'd be doing a little bit better if we didn't live in the city and had more affordable rent, but we'd scored with this place, and we had no intention of giving it up. It was safe, clean, and in a good neighborhood. The two of us paid our bills on time and still had money left over to have fun on weekends—when I wasn't studying or in the emergency room.

"I know you don't need it. But you'd get out of debt a whole lot quicker than you would otherwise. I know you've already had to start paying it back. I get our mail."

I nodded because school loans waited for no one and nothing before you had to start breaking the bank each month. The idea of having them paid off was more than a little tempting. I never minded the debt that medical school put me in because I knew it would be worth it in the end, and it was part of what I had to do to become a burn specialist.

"Starting my career debt-free does have a nice ring to it," I mumbled out loud instead of to myself, like I had intended.

Kayla leaned in closer to me, her phone in her hand. "Here, look at him. You haven't even looked at him."

Refusing to look at her phone, I looked everywhere else instead. "I've seen him a million times, unfortunately."

Over the last three years, I'd seen more pictures of Joseph Martin than I'd ever cared to. Although any female in her right mind would be asking to see pictures of him every single day until she died. Clearly, I was out of mine. But, he had done that. Made me hate him.

"You haven't seen him lately," she added before shoving her phone in front of my face, so close that I couldn't see anything, except for blurry blobs of color.

I moved her hand a safe distance away, and my heart literally leaped into my throat at the visual.

Stupid heart. Stay where you belong.

"He's gorgeous."

"He said the exact same thing about you," she said with a sly grin.

"Stop trying to butter me up."

"I'm not. He really did say that."

I hated that one look at his picture had me actually considering doing this. Twenty seconds ago, I couldn't have cared less about his existence, and now, I was practically drooling on Kayla's phone.

When was the last time I had sex? I couldn't even remember. That was the issue. I blamed my girl parts for going all stupid at the sight of his dark scruff and blue eyes.

"This is not a yes, but what does he want? Or what does he need exactly?"

Kayla rubbed her hands together like she had just masterminded some sinister plot to take over the world. "He needs to show his mom that he's happy and in love. All without the actual love part, of course. But she won't be an easy sell, so you'd have to actually make it believable."

I felt ridiculous for even wanting to know more, but here I was, curiouser and curiouser. "Why can't he find someone else? I'm sure a guy like that has a million women at his beck and call."

"You'd think so, huh? He really doesn't. I mean, there're a couple of women he fucks, but you've seen what they call him in the press. Or at least, you've heard me tell you."

I nodded because I knew exactly what they called him.

"I'm familiar with the names."

"He doesn't want to give anyone the wrong idea. Or give them hope for a future he doesn't have time for. It needs to be an arrangement, and he's super uncomfortable with me hiring a firm that could do this instead."

"Can we go back to the *couple of women he fucks* part?" I asked, realizing that he was a typical male, no matter what Kayla said.

"I knew you'd get hung up on that." She brushed her hair back. "It's just sex. He doesn't even see them that often. Honestly, he's usually too tired."

"Hmm," I said, not believing her.

"I mean it, Sutton. He's not a power-hungry asshole even though he could be. He totally could be."

Most men in his position would be using all that power and influence in every way imaginable, and I found it somewhat endearing, albeit a little unbelievable, that Joseph didn't.

"How did I even come up in conversation in the first place? Did you start talking about this insane idea and think, *Wow, Sutton would be great?*" I asked through gritted teeth, and she started giggling.

"It wasn't like that at all. But once I did think of you, I wondered why I'd never thought of the two of you together before. I mean, the fake hating each other aside," she said, and I made a sound that stopped her short.

"It's not fake for me," I argued before realizing what she'd said. "Wait, why does *he* hate me?"

"I don't know. Something about you trying to burn his balls off."

I scoffed out loud and leaned forward. "Is that what he told you?"

"Apparently, there was a lighter that got a little too close to his nutsack," she said, and I shook my head.

"He asked for it," I ground out before clamping my mouth shut. Of course he'd only tell the part that had me looking crazy and not the whole story.

"Anyway"—she sounded annoyed—"you two have a lot in common, and I never realized it before. That's all. I think you might actually like each other once you get through the rest of your crap. Like, this arrangement might not actually be torturous for either one of you."

I closed my eyes for only a second, and I had to fight with everything in me to open them again. When I did,

Kayla was staring at me.

"Let me sleep on it. I'm too tired to even consider not hating that man right now."

"But you will consider it? Right?" She sounded desperate, and she knew it.

"If he doesn't convince his mom he's in love, then what? She won't give him the company? She'll keep all the shares and hold them over his head forever? Give them to a bastard sibling he doesn't know exists?" I asked, still not truly giving a crap about Joseph or his future.

Kayla rolled her eyes and huffed out a loud breath. "You read way too many romance books back in college. And I already told you. She's just worried about him. She's afraid that if he doesn't at least try, he'll never find someone to love, and all he'll have is work and nothing else. No mother wants that for their only son."

Fighting back a yawn, I said, "That's actually kind of nice. Of her. Not him. He's annoying."

"It is nice. She just wants him to be happy. And that's all he wants for her too. They both want the same thing for the other. But the only way she'll go live her life is if she thinks he's actually having one."

I sat in silence for what felt like a million years, my brain spinning in circles. “I don’t know,” was all I could come up with in the moment because I truly didn’t know. “I need sleep.”

“Fine. But this conversation isn’t over,” she said before pushing up from the couch and disappearing into her room.

When I heard her door shut, I got up and did the same.

WHEN I WOKE up the next morning, I was greeted by various pictures of Joseph taped up all over the apartment. Each one had something written on it in black Sharpie.

How can you resist this face? You could fake kiss it anytime you wanted, read the one on my door.

Down the hallway was a printed picture of a BIC lighter with a red *X* across it that read, *NO LIGHTERS*. That one actually made me laugh.

There were three more pictures of her boss—each one shirtless, mind you—with various things that I could do to the body parts if I agreed. It almost made me grab my vibrator, but I kept walking toward the kitchen instead.

Another picture of Joseph with his mom was on the fridge, asking why I wanted to *break the old woman's heart*. I rolled my eyes at that one. But when I opened the cupboard to grab my favorite box of cereal, Joseph's face covered the entire thing, and it had been renamed to *Joseph-O's*.

Kayla was never going to let me say no to this.

WHAT DID SHE SAY?

JOSEPH

I WAS ON pins and needles, waiting for Kayla to get into the office. I'd tossed and turned all night, delirious and hopeful that she'd get Sutton to agree to this crazy shenanigan. Then, I'd cringe, remembering my poor balls, and wonder what I was thinking. I'd turned into a basket case.

When she finally walked out of the elevator, I was standing there like a stalker, waiting with my arms folded.

"Jeez, obsess much?" she teased before handing me a cup of coffee from my favorite place.

That wasn't a good sign. Kayla didn't go around, getting me coffee without being asked, which meant that she was buttering me up for bad news.

"She said no," I said as I sipped, careful not to spill it

all over my jacket.

"Not exactly." She leveled me with a look before nodding toward my office, where we could talk more privately.

"Well, what did she say?" I asked the second the doors closed behind us.

"She didn't say yes," Kayla started and made a sound to stop me from launching into a speech she knew I'd give. "But she didn't say no either. She's still considering it, even if she acts like she isn't."

"What do you think she'll say?"

She started laughing. "Yes. Eventually."

"How do you know this?" I wondered as my heart rate finally started to normalize, and I moved to sit at my desk.

"I can be very persuasive," she said, a smile still plastered on her face. "But I almost forgot."

"What?"

"I told her you'd give her money." She braced for my response.

I blew out a half-annoyed breath. I'd already assumed that I'd be paying her for her services.

"We established that yesterday."

"But I said it was a lot of money." Her eyes widened with the words, and I felt my body tense.

"How much?"

Kayla shrugged. "I didn't mention a number. I just said it would be a lot."

"Is two hundred thousand enough?" I blurted out the first amount that came to my head before thinking.

"I think that's fair," she answered, and she actually meant it.

"Fair? You think two hundred thousand dollars is fair?" I almost choked on the saliva in my mouth. It seemed a hell of a lot more than just *fair*. "Do you know how many lighters she could buy with two hundred K?"

"No wonder she hates you," she ground out. "Anyway, I researched the firms last night, and you'd be paying close to that, if not more, depending on the number of events and who you ended up choosing. So, yeah, I think it's a fair amount." She huffed. "Plus, it will help sway her. That's not a number she could easily brush off. No matter how much she hates you."

I didn't know. I didn't know anything about Sutton, and I couldn't believe that I was actually pushing for this as hard as I was, but I needed her help.

"What else will we need to get her to agree?"

"I thought about this all night. We need to go over the schedule, so I can see how many events you plan on attending and when they are. Sutton's schedule is crazy, so for this to even work, she'd need to know exact dates and times."

"We can do that," I said before it all hit me. "Kayla?"

"Yeah?" She looked up from her coffee, her head crooked as she watched me.

"What if we can't pull it off?" Fear tore through me. "It won't work if she genuinely hates me as much as you say she does."

"She doesn't hate you," she said firmly. "She just *thinks* she does."

I shook my head because that wasn't any kind of logic that made sense to me at all.

"You two are basically the same person. Just one of you has a penis."

"No thanks to her," I spat, and Kayla laughed.

"Don't forget about my raise," she said before exiting my office, leaving me to worry on my own.

JUST SAY YES ALREADY

SUTTON

I'D ACTUALLY GOTTEN home before Kayla, and I was grateful for the reprieve. It gave me a little time to sit down and think about any questions I might have about this insane arrangement offer. I'd been contemplating everything that we'd talked about from the night before. At least, what I could remember of it. I'd spent most of the day trying to talk my way out of helping her boss for no reason other than just to be difficult … and the fact that I hated him.

But she'd mentioned money. Again, not that I needed it, but it would be nice to get out of debt twenty years earlier than I'd originally planned. If I said no, it would only be to prove a point. But I wasn't sure exactly what point I was trying to make or who exactly I was trying to make it to. I was being stubborn just for the sake of being stubborn, and I knew it. I could be that way sometimes.

When Kayla eventually sauntered through our front door, I watched as a grin spread across her face when she noticed the pictures of Joseph still plastered all over.

No, I haven't taken them down yet.

And, no, I'm not reading into why.

"He is nice to look at, right?" she said with a grin, and I gave a nonchalant shrug.

"I guess," I answered before adding, "I have some questions."

I decided to jump right in and get this over with. There was no use in delaying the inevitable. If I knew my best friend at all, an additional conversation about the topic was only moments away. And more than likely, Kayla had come home prepared, ready for battle.

Before I knew what hit me, Kayla was sitting down at our two-person kitchen table, insisting I did the same as she pulled out a file folder and opened it.

"I'm ready for your questions," she said as she rested her hands in front of her and leveled me with an innocent look.

"What would be required of me exactly?"

"He needs a date." She paused before adding more details, "The *same* date, to the events he attends during Social Month."

"And these events are all formal, yes?" I asked, knowing damn well that they were.

She nodded slowly. "Yes."

"Like fancy dresses and stuff, right?"

"Uh-huh. But Joseph has accounts all over the city, and you can buy whatever you want and put it on his charge card," she said before tapping a finger against her lips. "That's actually good. People will believe that you're really dating if he's buying you clothes."

"I have my own dresses."

"I know. And some of those might totally work. But there's no harm in getting a few new pieces, right?"

"I guess not," I agreed. "But I can't go to wherever he needs me to for thirty whole days. You know I'm busy." I sounded defensive, but my work was important, too, and I wasn't going to pretend like it wasn't.

Luckily for Kayla—and her jerk boss—my upcoming schedule would actually allow for this ridiculous potential plan. My shift would be changing soon due to doctor vacations, which would give me more leniency than ever for the next twenty days. I was still expected to be at work, of course, but I had been told that it would be more studying and attending lectures while my specific training doctors were away.

"Joseph never attends all the events. I talked to him already and found out which ones he wants to go to and which ones he thinks you should be with him at. For whatever reason, you wouldn't be required to attend them all. Here's the list," she said, pulling out a single sheet of paper from her file folder and pushing it across the table toward me.

I grabbed the printed calendar and started scanning the dates. It actually didn't look too overwhelming, to be honest. There were a lot of days with nothing in them. Just empty squares.

"What do you think?"

Glancing up at her, I answered, "It actually looks doable."

"Right?" She sounded so surprised. "I thought the same thing."

"I need to see him again," I started to explain. "I can't do this without making sure I can at least look at him without wanting to sew his mouth shut. His mom will never believe it otherwise. She'll see the venom in my eyes."

"I know." She shook her head before groaning. "I can't believe you still hate him after all this time."

I blew out a breath. "It's not like he ever apologized or anything. And he was a complete jerk to me that night."

"So you keep saying."

"Anyway …" I brushed off where she was trying to steer the conversation.

I knew that Kayla wanted to know exactly what had happened between Joseph and me, but I didn't want to tell her. She would make excuses for his behavior, like reminding me that he had been drunk and wasn't normally such an ass.

But he had been so rude. Insensitive. And unkind. Even if he was hammered, that was no reason to say the things he had to me.

"You said his mom would be a hard sell. What's she like?"

Kayla whistled before leaning back against the chair. “She’s smart. Observant. Is aware of far more than she lets on. You can’t let your guard down around her. Even if you don’t see her, she will be watching.”

“Damn, Kayla,” I groaned, second-guessing my decision after hearing all of that.

“Don’t get cold feet now.”

“I’m just not that good of a liar, and you know it.”

She whipped up a hand and held out one finger. “That’s not true. You lie to people all the time in your line of work.”

“Hey,” I argued.

“I just meant that you mislead. Give people a little hope when there might not be any. Tell them you did all you could when maybe you didn’t. Or maybe there wasn’t anything that could be done. You make people feel what you need them to in order to be okay with whatever happened to their loved one.”

I wanted to fight with her, but she wasn’t wrong. Maybe I was a better deceiver than I gave myself credit for. “Fair point.”

“And for the record, you haven’t even asked.” Kayla

folder her arms across her chest and waited for me to fall for her baited trap.

"Asked what?" I asked, giving her what she wanted.

"How much money he's going to pay you for being his fake girlfriend." Her face looked like she held the greatest secret in all the world.

"Don't say it like that. It makes me sound like a prostitute." I stuck my tongue out like I'd eaten something rotten.

"Well, this prostitute is getting two hundred thousand." Her eyes widened as she waited for my reaction.

I coughed and choked out the word, "Pesos?"

Kayla laughed. "Dollars, you idiot."

I was in a little over a hundred thousand dollars' worth of school debt. "All to make his mom go away and leave him alone?"

"No. All of this to make his mom happy," she clarified. "He's a good guy, Sutton. You'll see," she said.

I really wanted to believe her.

But I didn't.

FIRST—NO, SECOND IMPRESSIONS

JOSEPH

"SHE AGREED," KAYLA said with a shit-eating grin on her smug face.

Shit. The evil troll had actually said yes. That brought up a whole new set of considerations.

"We need a contract. I want everything in writing," I blurted out, and Kayla's grin turned into a grimace.

"I want to argue with you right now because it's my best friend we're talking about, but a contract would be the smart thing to do."

"That's why I'm the boss," I said with a smirk of my own.

"She did have one condition." Kayla pursed her lips together, and I wondered what it might be.

"Spit it out, Sanderson."

"She needs to see you again. She wants to make sure this can even work, and she won't sign anything or commit a hundred percent until you do."

I guess I'm not the only smart one here.

"That makes sense," I agreed.

"I was hoping you'd say that. You two have a reservation at one in the café downstairs."

"Thanks, Kayla."

"Don't thank me yet. She still hates you."

That was a reminder I hadn't needed.

PROMPTLY AT ONE p.m., I strode down into the café and searched for a red-haired raven. I knew she'd be easy to spot, and thankfully, she was. Sutton was already sitting down at a table for two near the back with as much privacy as the café could muster, which wasn't much. We'd have to talk quietly. I couldn't risk anyone overhearing what we were attempting to do.

As I neared her, her green eyes shot up and pinned me with just a look. Her mouth refused to twist into a smile of any kind, and I could tell that just seeing me was setting her off. Clearing my throat, I decided to use my best manners.

"May I?" I pointed toward the chair across from her because I was suddenly scared that she might hurt me if I didn't ask permission first.

"That is why I'm here," she said, her tone snarky.

My gut reaction was to be as defensive and brash as she was being, but I knew that wouldn't work. Any asshole behavior from me, and she'd storm out of here and never look back, and then I'd be back at square one. I couldn't let that happen. I'd be fucked without her.

When I noticed a server heading in our direction, I nodded my head and waved her off. She got the message, promptly turning around on her heels and making a beeline in the opposite direction.

"Thank you for coming. For even considering this crazy idea," I said quietly before looking around. There wasn't anyone I recognized, but that didn't mean our conversation was safe from prying ears or eyes.

She cocked her head to the side, as if sizing me up, before shaking her head. "I can't do this," she said before shoving her chair back and standing.

I reached out, desperate to make her stay, and my hand grabbed ahold of hers. Those green eyes shot lasers at where I touched her skin, and I pulled back quickly.

"Please sit. Don't go."

Sutton begrudgingly sat back down and scooted closer toward the table between us. "I still hate you," she admitted before she started laughing. "It's ridiculous, I know. But seeing you brings it all back."

Damn.

I hadn't expected that kind of reaction. Especially when I was sitting there, trying not to salivate all over the table at the sight of her. I remembered her being hot the first time we met, but she truly was a stunner.

"What can I do to change that?" I genuinely asked. I found myself not wanting her to despise my existence the way she obviously did. Even though she'd been the one holding a lighter at my junk that night, I started thinking that maybe, just maybe, I'd done something to deserve it.

"Be a different person."

"Ouch," I said out loud. "It has been two years. Maybe I've changed?" I suggested, and she laughed again, the melody going straight to my groin. I shouldn't have been as turned on by this woman as I currently was. Didn't my dick remember how she'd wanted to maim him?

"Doubtful."

"You're right." I decided not to lie. "I'm still the same. Any other ideas?"

"Go back in time and make sure it never happens?" she suggested with a slight grin, and I wanted to hate how hard she was making this, but I could see her facade starting to crack.

"Is there any way we can pull this off without you wanting to murder me in the process?" I asked, my tone genuine.

"I don't know. Kayla said that your mom's tough and she won't be fooled easily, and you make me ragey."

My mom *was* going to be a hard sell. She wasn't naive, and she paid attention to details that most of us never took the time to see.

"I make you ragey?" I asked, repeating the word I'd never heard until now.

"Yeah. Like stabby," she said, and I laughed a little, uncomfortable because I thought she meant it.

"We need to date for real," I blurted out.

Where the hell did that come from?

"We need to what?" Sutton's voice cracked as she reared her head back.

"Yeah," I said as I worked through the details in my mind. "We need to go out a few times before Social Month starts. We can't have our first date be at an event where hundreds of people and press will be watching our every move. Not to mention, my mom. We have to be better than that."

She leaned forward, her body language relaxing almost instantly, but she kept her mouth shut. Just when I thought she was going to fight me on the suggestion, she said, "That actually makes sense."

I couldn't believe that she was being so reasonable.

"Good. I can show you that I'm not the terrible guy you seem to think I am."

"And I can show you that I'm not an evil troll." She forced a fake grin and glared at me.

She was clearly still bitter about the night I barely remembered. I had no idea why she felt like she had every right to despise me but not vice versa. She'd been the crazy one, not me! But I decided not to fight with her anymore. I needed her on my side, not against me.

"I know you're not. You're sitting here right now. That makes you the opposite of evil."

"But still a troll, right?" She rolled her eyes, and I shook my head.

"You're gorgeous, and you know it."

She didn't believe me. I could tell she didn't. And when she glanced down at the watch on her wrist, I knew our time together was over.

"I have to get back to work."

She pushed to a stand, and for once, I actually felt helpless. I had no control over this woman, and we both knew it.

"I don't have your number," I said, sounding desperate, and she gave me a half-grin. It was better than nothing, and I decided I'd take it and consider it progress.

"Get it from Kayla."

"Don't think I won't," I threatened as she walked away, her ass shaking in a pair of tight white pants.

Fake arrangement or not, I'd be getting into those.

HERE GOES NOTHING

SUTTON

I HATED HOW attracted I was to that man. But it was hard not to be. He was gorgeous. Confident. And he needed my help. Something about a man genuinely needing you and being aware of it was a jolt of power like nothing else. I had the upper hand in this fake arrangement, and I enjoyed that position.

Even though I'd almost walked out of our quick meeting more than once, I eventually settled down. Seeing him at first had reminded me of how awful he'd been when we met. But it was clear that he had very little memory of that night. If he had remembered it at all, he would have apologized or acted a little differently. That was the only reason I sat back down when he begged me too.

When he'd suggested going out before Social Month even started, I'd wanted to throw something at his face, but the more I thought about it, the more sense it made. The only way we'd be able to sell the idea of us dating would be if we actually started doing just that.

I needed to remember that it was all fake. That I was getting paid to go out with him, no matter what happened or how he acted. My being by his side would be purely for show, for the sake of his mom, and it wouldn't mean that Joseph Martin really wanted to be with me.

That was going to be the hardest part. Not because I planned on falling for the guy or anything, but because I was a female, and even though I had professional goals and aspirations that were my priority, I was still emotional. My heart wasn't a machine the way my brain was.

I had to keep it together … *somehow*.

JOSEPH GOT MY number from Kayla, like he'd promised to do, and started texting me that night. The first thing he wanted to know was my schedule for work and when we could go out publicly. He said the sooner we made our debut, the better. I responded to him, taking my time and making sure I didn't jump at his beck and call, but it was hard not to give him my full attention when no other man was even clamoring for it. At least, no man that I was interested in.

"He wants to go out tomorrow night," I said as I plopped down on the couch next to Kayla, who dropped the magazine she had been flipping through to look at me.

"Okay? So, what's the problem?"

"I don't know," I said, suddenly nervous and wondering what the hell I'd gotten myself into.

"No." Kayla's tone grew serious. "You're not getting cold feet now. You have to at least try."

"This isn't a good idea. You know it's not," I started to argue, but Kayla shook her head, her lips pursing together.

She cleared her throat before taking my hands in hers. "At least do the first dinner. The whole point of going out now is to see if it will work or not."

I swallowed around the lump in my throat. "You're right. I can do this. It's just dinner."

"And press," Kayla whispered.

I wasn't sure I'd heard her right or not.

"Did you say the press will be there?"

She winced slightly. "I am going to be calling the paps to anonymously report seeing him with a date." My mouth opened in disbelief as she continued, "I was going to tell you. It's fine. It won't be a big deal, but, Sutton, this is part of the arrangement. You'll be fine."

"How can you be so sure?" I suddenly felt like I couldn't handle any of this. Not dinner. Not the press. Not even being in Joseph's presence under the pretense that we were dating and, what … in love?

"Because there's two hundred thousand non-pesos riding on it."

Kayla's words hit me like a two-by-four to the side of the head. I'd already forgotten about the money. I nodded toward her, pulled myself together, and walked back into my bedroom to tell Joseph that dinner tomorrow was a go.

I HAD NO idea what the hell to wear even though I knew where we were going. I'd never been there, of course. The restaurant was not only out of my budget, but also out of my fun zone. It wasn't the kind of place you went to have a good time and let loose. For whatever reason, this dinner in the public eye had me squirming.

I looked at the pile of clothes that now covered my floor and almost called the whole thing off. The biggest issue was that I wanted to look like I belonged on Joseph's arm, but I also wanted to feel like myself, and I wasn't sure how to merge the two into one.

Blowing out a breath, I picked up the black cocktail dress from the floor and put it back on. It was form-fitting, hugging my curves without being too revealing. With the right necklace and a pair of earrings, I could dress it up a little more. Kayla came bursting through my door without knocking and let out a whistle.

"Oh, damn. You sure you want to date Joseph and not me?" she said, and I laughed.

I loved Kayla but only as a friend even though, sometimes, I wondered if it would be easier to date a woman. Then, I remembered all of Kayla's horror stories and realized that we were all equally screwed up and that dating was hard.

"It's okay?"

"You look stunning. It's perfect. He'll be here in ten."

"Okay," I said before spraying some hair spray into my hair. I'd curled it earlier, and the subtle waves were already falling out. I touched up my eye makeup, darkening my smoky eyes a tad more, which made the green color stand out.

For some reason, I seemed to be working really hard to impress him. I'd be lying to myself if I said I was doing it for the press. I knew that I wasn't.

Our door buzzed, and I heard Kayla press the button for the intercom before telling Joseph I'd be right down.

"Your knight in shining armor has arrived," she announced, and I rolled my eyes.

"If only," I mumbled in response. Joseph was not my knight.

I held on to the railing as I walked down the five flights of stairs. Our apartment didn't have an elevator, and walking in heels definitely wasn't my strong suit. When I reached the bottom, I could see Joseph standing outside of the glass doors, looking inside. His eyes widened when he caught sight of me, and my heart sped up at his reaction.

Down, girl. We're not involved in this, remember? Plus, we still hate him.

I opened the door, and he held out a single red rose for me to take.

"You look beautiful," he said before planting a kiss on the side of my cheek.

He made it hard to continue holding a grudge. He looked gorgeous, too, decked out in a charcoal-gray suit, no tie, and the top button undone on his shirt. The man had no right being that sexy.

The sound of clicking grabbed my attention, and I spotted someone holding a camera not too far away from us. So, that was why Joseph was being all gentlemanly and kind. We were being watched. I forced a smile, took his hand when he offered it, and headed toward the back of a black town car.

"Did you see that guy taking pictures?" I asked, assuming that he had.

"No." Joseph suddenly looked shocked. "Are you sure?" he asked. He looked around at the neighborhood as the car pulled away.

Now, he had me questioning my own judgment. Maybe the man hadn't taken pictures of us at all. Maybe I'd imagined things because Kayla had planted the seed in my head.

"I could be wrong," was all I managed to say in response.

"You probably aren't." He shifted in the seat next to me, angling his body toward me. "Are you ready for this?"

I swatted the butterflies flapping in my stomach. "For what exactly?"

"People paying attention. Watching what we eat. How we eat. How we act with one another. If we laugh. If we don't. Everything about this date is about to be under the microscope." His eyes pulled together, as if he was worried about me. Maybe he was.

"Can you ever be ready for all that?" I asked because if I overthought it, I wouldn't get out of the back of this car.

He laughed, and I enjoyed the sound far more than I had any right. There were only a few paparazzi hanging outside of the restaurant, but their attention was focused on us—more specifically me when they realized who I was with. The sound of Joseph's name being yelled was all I heard until he reached for my hand and navigated us inside. The maître d' was clearly expecting our arrival and escorted us toward the back, menus in hand.

Some heads turned to follow our movements, their eyes wide as Joseph continued to hold my hand for everyone to see. Other people couldn't have cared less who we were or what we were doing there. I liked that much better than all the attention.

Once we sat down, it was easy to forget about anyone else and focus solely on my fake date. Joseph became the one constant. Paying attention to him and no one else seemed to calm me. Even though he should have had the opposite effect.

"Tell me about your work at the hospital," he said as he perused the menu after a "complimentary" appetizer tray was brought out. "Your focus, I mean. You're in trauma?"

I shook my head. "I am, but that's not my specialty."

"What is then?" His fierce eyes met mine and held. "I should know this stuff about my girlfriend," he added, and I realized then that he didn't care about me personally. He was only doing his part of the job.

"The burn unit," I said, feeling confident and proud of my decision. That was, until his expression dropped and he looked down at his pants.

"Is that why you tried to light my junk on fire at the party?"

An annoyed sound escaped my lips. "For the last time, I wasn't trying to light you on fire."

"Well, someone was," he said in response.

I leaned back in my chair, my lips pursed together as I gave him a smug look. "You're right about that. Someone was."

He caught on to what I was hinting at instantly, and his mouth twisted into a smirk. "Are you saying that I was trying to light myself on fire?"

"If the shoe fits."

The waiter chose that moment to walk up and take our drink orders. I still hadn't looked at the menu long enough to decide and readily agreed when Joseph offered to pick for me. Our waiter disappeared, and Joseph narrowed his gaze on me again.

"So, why the burn unit? What about that drew you to it?" He folded his arms on top of the table, his focus solely on me, as if no one else existed in the room. Hell, the universe. That was how Joseph Martin made you feel when he watched you.

His question was something I thought about every single day. The patches of messed up tissue and skin grafts were all that remained on my body from a night I barely even remembered anymore. I ran my hand across my stomach before deciding that I'd tell him the truth.

"I got burned when I was a kid. My shirt caught on fire, and even though my parents got the fire out fast, I still had really bad burns on my stomach."

He hadn't expected that answer. I could tell by the look on his face.

"How did it happen?"

"Fireworks. And some stupid boys from the neighborhood." I honestly didn't remember the details anymore and only knew what my parents had told me.

"How old were you?"

"Six."

He held my stare as he breathed in and out five times. I counted, watching his chest rise and fall before he finally spoke. "Are you scared of fireworks now?"

A small laugh tumbled past my lips. No one had ever asked me that. "No. I enjoy them but only from a safe distance."

"Did the doctors save you that night?"

The waiter reappeared with our drinks, and we offered each other a cheers before taking a sip. He had ordered me some sort of red-blend wine that had been chilled and was exploding in my mouth.

"I've never had red wine chilled before," I said, and he smirked. I wanted to reach out and run my hand across his jawline but refrained.

"It's not a typical practice, but I prefer it that way," he said, "even though most people say I'm drinking it wrong."

I giggled. Actually, freaking giggled. "I'm not sure there's a wrong way to drink good wine."

"I'm glad you like it." He took another sip before placing it down in front of him. "You didn't answer my question about the doctors. Did they save you and that's what made you want to become one?"

"The doctors did save me. And I'm still self-conscious about the burn area. You'll never see me in a bikini or a crop top."

"I bet no one but you would even notice," Joseph said, and it was a sweet notion, but it was a lie.

My mind tossed me back in time to being a teenager and having my first boyfriend. I remembered the look on his face when his hands had run across my bare stomach, and apparently, it didn't feel right. He lifted my shirt without asking, looked underneath, and asked me what the hell happened to my skin. He wasn't kind or understanding. He'd been disgusted and a blabbermouth, telling everyone at school that something was wrong with me and they should stay away unless they wanted to catch "shark skin."

Up until a few years ago, that was exactly how a part of me had always felt—disgusting and different. Med school had changed all that for me. I was always grateful that I'd been saved as a kid and that the grafts had worked, but I'd never truly felt pretty in my own skin. Learning all about our bodies and the miraculous things they could do to heal themselves made me feel something new entirely about what mine had done for me. Sure, I had some imperfections, but who didn't? And being alive was worth the scars.

As the night went on, Joseph became my lifeline in a sea where I might have otherwise drowned—the constant stares, the not-so-stealthy cell phone photographs, et cetera. He made being with him easy, effortless, and I almost forgot that what we were doing wasn't real, that this wasn't a true first date with a man who wanted to get to know the real me because we hoped we could fall in love one day.

Ugh. My feelings were already messing with my head, and I realized in that instant that they were going to be hard to control.

IT'S NOT REAL

JOSEPH

THE IDEA THAT Sutton had been burned as a kid and dealt with scars her whole life … *affected me*. I could tell that she was hurt. Or had been hurt in the past. Most likely by idiot guys who were too stupid and shallow to see past the marks on the outside of her body and look inside. It didn't take much work to know that Sutton was smart, driven, ambitious and fucking awesome. She was nothing like I'd always thought she was—an evil fire-starting troll.

So, I sent her a text message the moment she walked through the doors of her apartment building, thanking her for the incredible evening. She responded immediately, and I knew that we were both feeling the same kinds of things. I'd actually enjoyed myself with her, forgetting half the time that I was paying her to do this favor for me.

Our date had felt so natural, not forced in any way. It had been genuine and good.

But it wasn't, and I needed to remember that.

All of this was a facade, a charade, a game we were playing, where I needed to keep a level head in order to win.

THE NEXT MORNING, I woke up to pictures of Sutton and me all over *Page Six*, the actual newspaper and online. My phone had blown up overnight, but I'd silenced it. If I didn't do that each night, I'd never get any sleep.

A text from my mom stood out at the top of my list.

Is this the woman you've been dating? She's quite beautiful. And familiar.

I wanted to say yes, but Sutton still hadn't officially agreed to attend Social Month with me. We hadn't signed any contracts or made any arrangements. The last thing I wanted to do was jinx it, so I didn't respond at all, knowing that I'd have to deal with her wrath later.

When I stepped off the elevator, both my mother and

Kayla were waiting for me.

"Not now, Mom." I tried to wave her off, but she shot me a nasty look.

"I remember where I know her from," she announced like she was about to win some kind of prize before throwing Kayla an inquisitive look, to which Kayla completely ignored. That girl was the one who deserved a prize.

"Is that so?" I tried to play it cool, but I felt myself grow more than a little nervous. My mom could be scary sometimes.

I blew them both off, continued walking into my office, and sat down at my desk before pulling up my emails, trying to give off the impression that I didn't have time for this, but my mom refused to let it go. She came right inside and closed the doors behind her.

"It's Kayla's friend. Am I right? The redhead?" She cocked her head to one side and waited for my response as my eyes met hers.

I actually didn't want to confirm it for her, feeling like she might figure out it was all some kind of scam and stop it before we even started.

"It is."

"Interesting," she deadpanned.

"And why is that interesting?" I refocused back on my computer, avoiding her gaze.

"Because I remember your last encounter with one another. It didn't go well." She laughed. My mom actually laughed.

I wondered how much of that interaction she'd truly seen that night.

"That's in the past. It was all a misunderstanding," I lied and hoped that she'd buy it.

"Mmhmm."

"Mom, can we talk about this later? I'm really busy."

"I'm just saying," she started, "I remember seeing a flame very close to your nether regions that evening."

"Mom!" I shouted, wanting this conversation to end.

"I'm only wondering why you didn't mention her before now, is all. How long has this been going on?"

Exhaling a loud, annoyed breath, I looked at her once more before figuring out what to say that she'd believe. "It's new."

"And you've forgiven her for trying to light you on

fire?" she pushed.

I grew more than a little anxious, thinking she had some sort of mom-like superpowers that she could wield at any moment and see through my bullshit.

"I told you," I breathed out again, "it was a misunderstanding."

She made a clicking sound with her tongue. "Don't try to fool me, Joseph. If this thing between you two isn't real, I'll know," she warned as she opened my door and stepped out of it just as Kayla threw herself in.

"Not you too," I groaned, and Kayla shushed me.

"We need to make some kind of statement," she said quietly, and I folded my hands on top of my desk and stared at her.

"What do you mean?"

"You two went public last night. You haven't done that since college." She gave me a pointed look.

I hadn't needed the reminder. "I know that, Kayla."

"She's already getting harassed," she breathed out.

I felt my back stiffen and my protective nature burn to life.

"Tell me everything," I demanded.

"I don't know much, but she said there were paparazzi outside of the hospital this morning when she went in. Her emails are filled with media requests, and they have been calling her work nonstop."

I didn't need to hear any more to know how bad this was. How annoyed Sutton would be that her personal life was interfering with her work. She'd filled me in on her job last night, her face lighting up whenever she talked about all the people she wanted to help. It gave her control in a world filled with chaos. I recognized her passion. And I respected it.

"She's going to bail on me before we get started," I said, suddenly concerned that I'd lose this woman before I even had her.

Wait. Lose her? She's not mine, I reminded myself.

"That's why I was thinking that we should make some kind of statement. We confirm the relationship but ask that the media please refrain from stalking your girlfriend at her place of employment," Kayla suggested.

Before I considered what a statement like that might do, I nodded my head and waved her away.

Reaching for my cell phone, I fired off a text to Sutton,

apologizing and asking her if I could make it up to her tonight. I didn't expect her to respond since she was at work already, so I wasn't surprised when she didn't. But when four hours had passed and there was still no message from her, I pulled up my texting app and realized that it hadn't been delivered yet.

She must have turned her phone off.

'Cause everyone was fucking harassing her.

I grabbed my things and stormed out of my office as Kayla yelled, "Where are you going?"

"I'll be right back," I growled. "Pull the car up."

"You have a meeting in twenty minutes!" She chased after me as I stepped into the elevator without her.

"Guess I'll be late," I said as the doors closed, shutting Kayla's worried face out of my view.

I drove like a maniac, pissed off, possessive, and concerned. When I got to the hospital, I hopped out of my car and walked through the front doors like I owned the place, pretending not to see the handful of press still hanging around. They went nuts when they saw me there, shouting my name and hers.

"Where is Sutton?" I asked the nurse who was

watching me through narrowed eyes from behind a sheet of Plexiglas.

"I know who you are," she said, but her tone told me she was not a fan.

"I'm sure you do. Can you page her? I need to see her. Now."

"You've turned our hospital into a circus." She shook her head, but I saw her reach for the phone and linger over the intercom button. "Take the elevator up to floor three and meet her at the nurses' station there. Otherwise, those people will never leave."

I knew better than to argue with her, so I did as she'd demanded, practically sprinting for the bank of elevators before pressing the button a hundred times in rapid succession, as if doing that would make it come quicker. When I stepped through the doors on the third floor, Sutton was leaning over a desk, talking to one of the nurses, her long red hair tied back into a ponytail that had me thinking dirty thoughts.

I moved in her direction; she still hadn't noticed me, but other women had started to.

"Hey," I breathed out, and she whirled around quickly,

her eyes widening with surprise.

"What are you doing here?" She grabbed my sleeve and pulled me away from the desk, which was now filled with smiling nurses and who I assumed were doctors.

"You're really not going to introduce us?" one of them shouted, and Sutton's cheeks turned red as she ignored the request, still pulling me around a corner.

Once we stopped moving, I looked right at her and said, "I was worried." My hands had started shaking by that point because I was so riled up, so I stuffed them in my pockets.

Sutton tugged on my arm once more, moving us into a room where a few small bunk beds sat, perfectly made.

"Is this a real-life on-call room?" I asked because I had very little knowledge of hospitals aside from things I'd seen on TV.

"What? Oh, yes, it is. Joseph, what's wrong? Why are you here?" She looked worried … *for me.*

I stepped forward, closing the distance between us before I reached for her shoulders and tucked an errant piece of red hair behind her ear. Her eyes closed with my movement, and it took everything in me not to bend down and start kissing her.

"I needed to see that you were okay. I heard about the press and the phone calls," I tried to explain, but I wasn't sure my words were coming out right.

She swallowed hard, her eyes avoiding mine. "It's been a lot," she said softly. "I wasn't prepared."

Shit. She's going to walk away. She's going to say this is too much for any sane woman to handle, and then I'll be back to square one. And I really, really, really don't want to start over. At least, not without her by my side. What the hell is wrong with me?

"How can I help? What can I do to fix this?" I asked, genuinely meaning it.

She shook her head and gave me a one-armed shrug. "It's not really your fault. I can handle it." She inhaled. "I just wasn't expecting that level of things, was all. I'll be better prepared next time."

A small, confident smile appeared out of nowhere, and I reached out, my thumb brushing along her bottom lip. She sucked in a breath as she pulled away, and I apologized like I'd done something wrong or out of line.

"I'm not okay with you being uncomfortable or

harassed in any way. Do you understand that?"

"Sure," she said, but I could tell she wasn't getting it. At all.

I was already possessive over her, and her safety was quickly becoming a top concern.

"Sutton," I growled under my breath, "I wanted to rip their fucking heads off."

"Whose heads?"

"The press. Every single one of them standing outside of your hospital right now. I sent you a text, and you didn't answer, and I lost my fucking mind."

She shifted on her feet. "My phone is in my locker. I turned it off."

"I noticed."

The realization finally hit her. "That's why you're here? Because I didn't answer a text?" She sounded annoyed instead of happy.

"I was worried," I bit out.

I was right; she wasn't amused.

"Well, I'm fine. You can't come storming in here whenever you want and demand to see me because I didn't jump at your beck and call. Just so you know, I turn my phone off a lot when I'm at work."

Stepping away from her, I dragged my fingers through my hair, frustrated. "Why are you so mad at me right now?"

"I don't know," she ground out before pulling at her ponytail and tossing it over her shoulder.

"Well, can you figure it out before dinner tonight?" I said, clearly catching her off guard.

"Dinner? Again?"

"Don't sound so excited," I said, my tone harsh.

"Sorry." She shook her head but kept her distance. "I can't go tonight."

"Why not?" I found myself feeling way more disappointed than I had any right to be.

" 'Cause I have to work late," she said, and I knew she wasn't telling me the truth.

I could have pushed her harder, told her that I knew she was full of shit, and forced her to go out with me again, but I didn't want to do that. I took a step in her direction and watched as she straightened her back and swallowed, her lips pressing together as I neared.

"You're lying. But I'll let it go. For now."

"How gracious."

That smart mouth was going to get her in trouble at some point. Most likely sooner rather than later.

"Are you playing a game with me, Sutton?" Something started to gnaw at me, like maybe she was going to pull out before Social Month even started and leave me high and dry.

"What do you mean?"

"Nothing. Make sure we can go out again soon." I stormed out of the room before I did something stupid, like throw her onto one of those beds and have my damn way with her.

MEETING MOM

SUTTON

WHY THE HELL was I so irritated? Walking out of the on-call room and toward the nurses' station, I felt a ball of dread in my stomach. Everyone was watching me, their eyes filled with mischief, wonder, and accusations.

"He's gorgeous," one of the women said as I approached.

I turned around just in time to see Joseph disappear into an elevator.

"I know. I know," I agreed before I continued moving down the hall.

If I stopped for even a second too long, I'd never get away from all the questions, and the last thing I wanted to do was lie to all their faces. I'd already done that this morning after the pictures of me and Joseph from last night went viral and the press showed up.

I spent the rest of the afternoon trying to figure out what my problem was, but I was no closer to the truth than I had been an hour before. Joseph showing up, all concerned for my well-being and over-the-top dramatic, had messed with my head. His actions had felt like something a real boyfriend would do, but he wasn't my boyfriend. He wasn't anything, except for a paycheck at the end of my service.

I shook out my body after thinking those words to get rid of the icky feeling it had given me. My accepting a paycheck for this seemed weird and wrong. But I still planned on doing it.

"Sutton, you're still here?" Dr. Bonnova asked as we passed each other in the hallway.

She was a freaking goddess at this hospital, all groundbreaking and ridiculously smart. It was awesome that she even knew who I was.

"Yes?" I asked, clearly confused.

"It's almost seven," she said, and I reared back my head.

"Oh." I'd spent so much of the day lost in my own

thoughts that I didn't even realize I'd stayed past my assigned shift. "Thanks, Dr. Bonnova. Have a good night."

She laughed as I picked up my pace. "Have fun with Romeo's Other Brother," she shouted, using one of his less popular nicknames from the press.

I spun on my heels, turning around to face her, but she waved me off, and I swallowed whatever words I was going to say instead of saying them out loud. Then, I reminded myself that I needed to get used to this kind of thing. If I was going to be fake dating Joseph Martin, I had to be prepared for everything that came with it, and that included comments from my coworkers who were all too familiar with his reputation in the city.

And that was why I'd been so irritated when I saw him earlier. I wasn't really pissed that I'd been harassed since the moment I woke up, that my voice mail was filled, and that my social media accounts had been inundated with requests and direct messages. I wasn't even mad that the press and paparazzi had found out where I worked and shown up there, waiting to get pictures of me. I mean, one night with Joseph had turned my life into something I hadn't even remotely considered. I'd thought I understood what being seen with him meant, but I had no clue.

To be fair, none of that was any of his fault or choice. What I was mad about was the fact that he'd come over to my place of employment and pretended to care about my well-being and mental state. He acted like I mattered when we both knew that I didn't. He showed up in the middle of the day to check on me. And it'd made me so angry because ... *I liked it.*

And I wanted it to be real.

Walking into the locker room, I grabbed my phone and turned it on for the first time since I'd turned it off that morning. Alerts pinged for what felt like a full five minutes before finally stopping. I looked down at the screen and couldn't believe the number of notifications there. I opened my text messages first. The social media requests could wait. I scrolled through, responding to my parents separately before stopping on Joseph's name.

He'd sent another text about an hour ago.

UH, MY MOM HAS REQUESTED OUR PRESENCE.

My heart dropped inside my chest, and I almost let go of my phone. Instead of texting him back, I pressed on his name and called him.

"Hey," he answered on the first ring.

"I just got your text. What?"

"She wants us to come over. She's insisting."

I sat down on the long bench, thankful that no one else was in the room. "When?"

"Now?" he said like it was a question.

I blew out a long breath. "Are you kidding me?"

"I know. I tried to blow her off, but if we don't do it tonight, we'll have to do it tomorrow. Let's just get it over with. Please? I'll make it up to you."

He sounded desperate. Or maybe he was just tired and didn't have the kind of energy to argue with his mother, knowing that he was going to lose.

"I need an hour," I begrudgingly agreed. It had already been such a long day, and I was exhausted.

"I'll see you in thirty."

He ended the call, and I wanted to throw my phone against the wall. Or "accidentally" drop it in the sewer on my way home.

I GROANED OUTWARDLY when the buzzer at my apartment

let me know that he had arrived in thirty minutes, like he'd said, instead of listening to me.

"I'll buzz you up, but I'm not ready," I said into the intercom before pressing the button to allow him to enter the building.

I hadn't even told Joseph my apartment number, but he must have known it from Kayla because a loud knock on the door had me shouting for him to just come in. Peering around the hallway corner, I watched the door swing open, and Joseph stepped through the threshold, his eyes catching mine immediately.

"You can't just invite people inside, Sutton. What if I were a murderer?"

"I would do my best to defend myself then."

"Please be safer," he said, sounding irritated as he looked around our living space.

"Let me finish getting ready."

I was relieved to see him wearing a pair of jeans and a tight-fitted T-shirt. I'd wanted to dress casual, too, for the meeting with his mother, but I hadn't been sure if his family even believed in the term.

"Joseph, help yourself to anything in the fridge," I

shouted, but he stayed quiet. I assumed he was on his phone, handling work emails, but I almost screamed when I looked in the mirror and saw his reflection behind me. "What are you doing?"

"I wanted to see what was taking you so long." He stepped into the small space, both of our bodies barely fitting.

"Stop being a creeper," I complained, pushing him out of the bathroom. "Out."

He grinned. He liked the challenge. "I like this color on you." He fingered the sleeve of my cream-colored sweater.

"What is tonight going to be like?" I asked as I attempted to straighten my hair. It had been up in a ponytail all day long, so there was a bump at the top that I was trying—and failing—to tame.

"I honestly don't know. I haven't brought a woman home to meet my mom since college."

"You're kidding."

"I'm not."

"What if she sees through us? I mean, we need a plan." I was starting to get nervous.

"Like an escape plan?" he asked with a grin, and I narrowed my eyes at him. "One where you fake an emergency and bail?"

"No, not like that." I let out a slight laugh. "Women ask a lot of questions. We live for details. She's going to want to know how we met, how you asked me out, how we started dating." I started running off a list of things that I'd want to know if it were my son bringing home someone new for the first time.

Joseph stepped back into the tiny bathroom, his body pressing against mine, and I willed my heart to stop pounding against my chest, scared that he might be able to feel it.

"We'll get our stories straight in the car ride over."

God, he smelled good. And those lips. I wanted to know what they felt like, what they tasted like, and how they kissed.

My voice got lost in my throat, so I nodded my answer instead.

"Hello? Sutton? Where are you?" Kayla's voice broke our mutual trance, and Joseph practically fell out of the bathroom door and into the narrow hallway right as Kayla appeared. "Why are you two in the bathroom together?"

"Your boss was trying to intimidate me," I said before wondering where those words had come from.

"I bet he was," she said, wagging her eyebrows.

"If I didn't come back here, she'd never finish getting ready," Joseph added, and I put the finishing touches on my makeup before declaring that I was done.

"Where are you guys going?" Kayla asked, her face pinched together, as if she hadn't expected us to have another fake date so soon.

"Apparently, his mother wants to see us," I said, choking on the words.

"She what?" Kayla whirled around and faced Joseph. "Joseph! You're throwing Sutton into the lion's den already? Your mother is going to eat her alive."

"Thanks for the vote of confidence," I said, suddenly worried that I was going to sweat through my shirt.

"You've been out one time!" she practically screamed. "I'm telling you, that woman has superpowers."

"Sutton will be fine," Joseph said. "See you tomorrow, Kayla."

He placed his hand on my lower back as I walked out

of the bathroom and down the hall. I turned around, meeting Kayla's eyes, and I knew she sensed what I was feeling without me needing to say it.

I was in trouble.

I was going to fall for this man, and we both knew it.

That was, if I made it through the night with his mother.

ALREADY FALLING

JOSEPH

WE SAT IN the back of a town car, my driver heading toward my mother's penthouse.

Once we were buckled in, Sutton turned to face me. "We really need to get our stories straight."

"You're right," I agreed, and we worked out a few details—making up some bullshit story about how we had run into each other one night, recognized one another, and I'd asked her out on the spot—before arriving at the front of my mom's building and pulling to a stop.

"We're already here?" Sutton looked nervous.

"We'll just play it by ear. She's not going to grill you until you crack," I tried to reassure her, but honestly, I had no idea what my mother was capable of or what she planned on doing.

Kayla wasn't wrong when she said the woman had superpowers. She definitely did.

"She won't leave you alone unless you're in love. Have you forgotten that small detail?"

Apparently, I had. "What's your point?"

"We are not in love. We barely even know each other."

"It will be fine," I said again before I stepped out of the car before moving to get her.

"Good evening, Mr. Martin," the doorman said as we neared.

"Evening, Alexander," I said in response as he held the door open for us.

We walked to the bank of elevators, and I pressed the button. We stepped inside, and I swiped a card and hit the PH button.

"I'll let Mrs. Martin know you have arrived and are on your way up," Alexander said before the doors closed.

We rode up in silence. I held her hand without even thinking about it. I wanted Sutton to be calm, to realize that I wouldn't bring her to someone who was going to hurt her. Hell, I wanted her to trust me.

"Here goes nothing," Sutton said under her breath

when the elevator dinged and the doors opened into my mother's waiting area.

"Oh, Joseph. You're finally here!" My mother appeared from the sitting area, her hair and makeup perfectly done. "And this must be Sutton."

Sutton dropped my hand as she smiled, and it lit up the whole damn room. "I'm sorry we're late. It's my fault. I had extra patients to check in on at the hospital."

"Nonsense. You do important work. I can wait," Mom said with a smile of her own before planting a kiss on my cheek. "I'm glad you're both here. We need to talk about all the press you two are getting. They're asking me questions I can't answer, considering I haven't even met my son's girlfriend until now. Well, unless you count that one other time," she added with a wink, and Sutton turned bright red.

"Let's not," Sutton said, and my mother laughed.

"Agreed. Let's go into the sitting room," Mother directed.

Sutton shot me a look that told me she thought our house was over the top, but it was all I'd ever known. This shit was normal to me.

I reached for Sutton's hand, intertwining it in my own as we followed my mother through the doorway and into my favorite room in the house. The fireplace was lit, and the window shades were up, highlighting the city.

I used to sit in here and stare out the windows after my dad had passed, watching all of the New Yorkers wander around in a daze. It wasn't the same after 9/11 happened. We were broken, but it felt like we were all broken in the same way. I was lost then, but so was everyone else. For a moment, our world went dark; all the light was replaced with something hazy and blurred. Eventually, we'd all come back to life, together, in unison.

I felt a small tug on my hand, and I realized that Sutton had stopped walking. She was looking at the framed pictures on top of the fireplace mantel.

"Is that your dad?" She let go of my hand and leaned in close.

"Wasn't he handsome?" My mother's voice filled the air, a mixture of pride and sorrow.

I wondered how often she came into this room now that I no longer lived here.

"He was." Sutton stumbled on the past tense of the

word. "You look just like him."

I inhaled quick. It was sharp, and it stabbed. I knew I resembled him, but it had been a long time since anyone had said it out loud. Years maybe.

My mother moved to her reading chair, and I noticed there was a cup of tea sitting on the table beside it. She waved a hand toward the two-person lounge for us to take. Sutton sat first, and I sat unbearably close to her, our thighs pressing against each other, making my mind instantly wander. I placed my hand on top of her leg and left it there, trying to hide the fact that I wanted to move it all the way up until I landed on the place that would give her the most pleasure. That was what two people enamored with one another did, right?

"Do you want a drink? I can have something brought in," my mom asked as she sipped her tea.

Sutton shook her head. "I'm actually okay," she said, and I agreed because it seemed easier.

"Are your parents still married, Sutton?"

I didn't know the answer to the question my mom had asked, so I paid attention to Sutton's response, watching her nod at first before adding, "They are."

"How lovely. That's no small feat these days."

"They seem happy."

"Where are they? Here in New York somewhere?"

Sutton let out a laugh. "No. They live outside of Boston."

My mom's expression shifted slightly before she composed herself. If I didn't know her as well as I did, I would have missed it completely. But I noticed it all—the wince, the legs crossing and then uncrossing, the smile that appeared genuine but really wasn't. Sutton was an outsider who lived far away from her family.

"I take it, you don't see them very often?"

"Unfortunately, no. With my schedule at the hospital, I don't have many days off. And they both work."

"They must miss you."

"I miss them too," she said with a soft smile, and I leaned over, planting a kiss on her cheek. She looked surprised or caught off guard before her hand gripped my chin and her thumb ran across it like she'd done it a thousand times before.

"So, tell me, how'd you two meet? I mean, aside from that dreadful night at the gala."

“Mother,” I chastised her. Didn’t she promise to put that night aside?

“My apologies,” she said, but she wasn’t even remotely sorry.

She was up to something; I just had no idea what.

Sutton and I began the story we’d practiced on the car ride over. How we had run into each other at a bar one night.

“He was buzzed,” Sutton said, and I wanted to kick her ankle for the lie. “But that’s why he talked to me in the first place.”

“No,” I disagreed but figured it still sounded believable enough. “I knew I recognized her face, but I couldn’t place the where or why.”

“Then, Kayla came over to where I was, and apparently—” she said before I interrupted.

“It all clicked. The little fire starter.” I snapped my fingers, and Sutton growled, smacking my leg.

My mother laughed. She was actually smiling, listening to the two of us spout off this lie. “And then what? You asked her out, or did you make Kayla do the dirty work for you?”

"Kayla," Sutton said at the same time that I said, "I did."

We both sucked in a breath.

Sutton's eyes grew wide, but she quickly recovered. "You did not ask me out that night. You talked to Kayla the next day and sent her home with instructions for me."

"Instructions?" my mother questioned. "That's not very romantic, Joseph."

"She just means that I told Kayla that I wanted her phone number and to make sure she didn't say no," I explained.

"Even after the fire incident? I was under the impression that you two didn't like one another," my mother pushed. She clearly remembered more about that night than I did.

"That night was a big misunderstanding," Sutton said. "We're past it now."

"I can see that," my mother said as she reached for her tea once more and took another drink. "Is this thing serious? It must be if you're making public appearances."

Sutton's leg muscles twitched under my grasp, and I gave her a squeeze.

"It's getting there," I said.

"It's still new, but I like where it's heading." Sutton gave me a look, and either I misread her completely or I was too damn hopeful for my own good.

"So, I assume you're planning on bringing her to the Social Month events?" Mother directed that question at me.

"That is the plan," I agreed.

"And you're ready for what that will entail, Sutton? I mean, for you personally?" she asked, this time looking straight at Sutton, who I felt tense once again under my grasp.

Sutton cleared her throat and quickly glanced at me before focusing on my mother. "I think so. If today was any indication, I have a pretty good idea."

My mother grinned, but it wasn't necessarily pleasant. "Today was nothing compared to what will happen if you continue being seen together. Especially after Social Month. The press will hound you at every step. They'll camp outside your apartment door. They will talk to your coworkers at the hospital. They'll dig up your past, your present, your parents in Boston. They will want to know everything about the woman who has captured Not-So Prince Charming's heart."

"Mom," I chastised, not wanting her to scare Sutton half to death.

"No," Sutton said, stopping me. "She's right. It won't be easy. But I'm sure Joseph will do everything he can to keep me safe, and hopefully, they'll like me, so they won't be too mean."

Sutton was attempting to be lighthearted, but damn, she really had no idea how vicious the press and gossip columnists could be. Over the years, I'd learned, but I also didn't give a fuck. Sutton would care. She'd be hurt by the things they printed and wrote about her. Especially if she started reading the comments. Those were not for the faint of heart.

"It doesn't matter if they like you, dear. Being nice doesn't sell. It's not good for their business," my mother warned before covering a yawn. "I think I need to turn in for the night. I have some things I need to think over."

The three of us stood at the same time, and Sutton immediately reached for my hand and held it in a vise grip. My mother walked us to the elevator, and Sutton and I stepped inside. Right as the doors were about to close, my mother reached her arm out to stop them.

"It was really nice meeting you tonight, Sutton. This charade you two are trying to pull is cute, but you need to think long and hard about what you're getting yourself into. And you, my son, should know better than to throw someone into the spotlight without warning. Especially when it's all for show."

"What are you talking about?" I questioned, pretending to play dumb but I knew we were caught.

"You can't fool me, Joseph. I'm offended that you'd even try."

And just like that, she pulled her hand away, and the elevator doors slammed shut.

CRAP WITH A CAPITAL C

SUTTON

"SHIT," JOSEPH SAID as the elevator started going down.

"How did she know? I thought we did a good job," I asked, my hand still holding his for dear life.

His blue eyes were wild, roving all over the walls and my body. I could tell that his mind was spinning. "Probably the fact that neither one of us knew about the other's parents. That was the first dead giveaway that we hadn't talked about things that actually mattered."

"I didn't realize your dad had passed," I said softly, not wanting to cause him any more pain than necessary.

Joseph looked at me and said two words. "Nine eleven."

He didn't need to say anything else. Those words had

said it all, and my heart broke for him. Everything about that day had been devastating, even when you didn't know anyone personally affected by it.

When the elevator bounced to a stop at the ground level, I had no idea what we were going to do next. I wasn't sure that Joseph even wanted to go through with our arrangement anymore, especially now that his mom knew we were lying. And if I was being honest, the things she'd said scared me a little. I wasn't ready for my life to turn upside down, especially for someone who would eventually leave me to deal with it all on my own because none of this was even real.

Joseph walked ahead of me, still holding my hand, as we exited the building, and the chilled air hit us.

"Are you okay?" I asked.

He stopped walking and turned around to face me, his blue eyes appearing as dark as the night. "I don't know. Are you?"

"I'm a little rattled," I admitted, and he grinned.

I already loved seeing that grin … being the one who put it on his face. Literally a day into this arrangement with him, and I was already attached.

"Me too. But …" he started to say before looking around. The streets weren't empty, and people definitely recognized who he was as they walked past. "Want to go somewhere and talk, or do you want me to take you home?"

"Go somewhere," I said without taking a breath. I wasn't ready for this night to end. I probably never would be.

"I'll be right back." He dropped my hand and headed toward where the car was still parked, his driver inside. He leaned in through the driver's window before coming back in my direction, his hand extended toward me, waiting for me to grab it.

He was most likely going to take me somewhere public, so he could fake dump me and assure himself that I wouldn't make a scene. And that was when my heart cracked inside my chest a little, letting me know that it didn't want to be dumped. Fake or not. My heart and I liked being with him. Even though he still owed us an apology for that night years ago.

"It's right over here," he said as we walked down an alley toward a small restaurant I'd never been to before.

He pulled open the door and let me go in first before taking the lead again. We walked between the tables and chairs and straight into the back, through the kitchen. I had no idea what was happening, but when we reached a set of stairs that went down, I realized that was where we were heading. Down.

"Where are we going?" I asked, a little unsure of what could be underground.

"You'll see."

Joseph stopped in front of a door that resembled one of those old bank safes. I didn't even notice the buzzer on the wall until he moved his finger to press it. It lit up, and instantly, a secret window in the door slid open, and a pair of eyes stared at us.

Joseph opened his mouth to say something—I had no idea what—when the window abruptly slammed closed and the sound of a lock clicking echoed. The heavy door swung open slowly, and the man behind it bent down to give Joseph a hug. He was huge, as tall as he was broad.

"Good to see you. It's been a while," the burly man said.

"How's it look tonight?" Joseph asked, and I wasn't

sure exactly what he was referring to because I had no idea what we were about to walk into.

"Private," he said as he held the door open for us.

"Perfect."

When we stepped inside, the first thing I saw was how dark the space was. There were numerous light fixtures attached to the walls, but they must have been set on the lowest setting possible. The booths had extremely high backs, which I assumed were for privacy, and they were scattered in no logical order. The bar resembled an old Western movie with rich, deep woods and bottles on the shelves that honestly looked a hundred years old.

"What is this place?" I whispered.

Aside from the Frank Sinatra music that played over speakers you couldn't see, it was fairly quiet, and I didn't want to draw attention.

"A limited-access speakeasy," he answered, and I had no idea what that meant.

Once we sat down at one of the high-back booths, Joseph across from me, I realized that you really couldn't hear any of the conversations happening around you. Which meant that no one would be able to hear ours either.

"What's a limited-access speakeasy?" I asked.

A gorgeous woman appeared, almost out of thin air, to take our drink order. I had no idea what to get, so Joseph asked me what kind of hard alcohol I preferred.

"Vodka," I said in response. "Always vodka."

Once he ordered for me and she disappeared, Joseph leaned across the table separating us. "You know what a speakeasy is, I assume."

I nodded.

"A limited-access one is basically like a private club. Only certain people can come in here."

"Do you pay a fee?" I asked, genuinely curious. I'd never heard of such a thing before in my life.

"No. It's not like a country club. But you have to be invited and accepted. The whole point is to keep private business private."

"How do you get invited?"

"Word of mouth. Everyone who comes here is very powerful in their own way. But it isn't just money that gets you in. Usually, that's not enough. Your reputation counts. What you do for work. Who you do business with. All kinds of things," he said, and I nodded like this was a totally common thing.

"Are there any women members?" I asked, and his mouth turned up into a lopsided grin.

"Yes. Probably half are women," he answered just as Miss Gorgeous returned with our drinks.

Joseph held his glass of what I assumed was whiskey in the air between us, and I pressed mine against his before we both took a sip.

"Oh, this is delicious," I said, admiring the giant globe of ice in the middle and the scent of oranges.

"I'm glad you like it."

I leaned my back into the booth and took another drink. "Did you bring me here to fake dump me?" I blurted out.

Joseph's eyes bulged. "What? No. Why would you think that?"

"Because your mom called us out tonight. She knows we're faking."

He crossed his arms over his chest. "Does she though?"

Wait, what?

"I mean, she said it. She knows."

"She *thinks* she knows. And she tried to scare you off tonight. If we keep doing what we're doing, then at some point, she'll have to admit she was wrong," he explained.

I wasn't sure if it was the logic or the alcohol, but it all seemed to make perfect sense to me in that moment.

"So, we don't stop?" I said, my relief permeating every word.

"Not unless you want to." He leaned over the table again, his hands reaching out for mine. "Do you want to stop?"

"No," I admitted, and he grinned again. That damn grin. That damn face. I felt vulnerable with what I'd just said, so I asked him the same question. "Do you want to stop?"

"Never," he said, and I felt my heart jump.

"Don't say things like that," I warned.

"Or what?"

"Or I might fall in love with you for real."

"But you hate me, remember?" he reminded me, and I swallowed the pinprick of hurt that his response elicited inside of me.

"I did. I mean, I do. I mean, I don't know anymore." I

threw my head into my hands and closed my eyes for a second, wishing I could take back my words because they made me feel stupid.

He looked like he might spit out his drink. Like what I'd just said about falling in love with him for real was the most horrible thing in the world that could happen. But he was the one who had just said he *never* wanted to stop this thing between us.

Why are men so confusing?

"Have you eaten anything today?" he asked, and it only made me more annoyed.

But I thought back on the entirety of the day, and I'd been so stressed out that I wasn't sure I had.

"I can't remember," I answered honestly, and he gave me a look as if my response explained it all.

He waved a hand, and Miss Gorgeous was back, taking his order with a nod before leaving us alone once more.

"Maybe we should talk about that night," he suggested.

My first response was to argue with him and make him fight for it, but I acquiesced instead.

We needed to get it out in the open. Although I wasn't sure I'd be able to forgive him again if he still acted the same or defended the version I'd first met.

"Sure. Start talking."

I waited.

And waited some more.

But Joseph only sat there, staring at me.

"I don't know what to say."

"You could start with telling me you're sorry. Did it ever cross your mind to apologize?"

Rearing back, he swallowed a laugh before launching into some diatribe. "Me? Apologize to you? You're the one who wanted to burn off my manhood. You should be apologizing to me!"

"*I* wanted to burn off your manhood? *I* wanted to?" I stopped short, my anger grabbing hold of me. I hated that it felt like we'd just taken a million steps backward. "You were the one waving a lighter at your nuts that night. Not me. I took the lighter from you before you lit your damn pants on fire," I said.

He looked at me like I was a complete lying psychopath instead of the honest-to-God truth-teller that I was being.

"Why the hell would I ever do that?"

"Because you were being a jerk. You said that I was too pretty to be a surgeon. You asked me if I was sure I didn't want to be a trophy wife instead. You were insulting and degrading, and you wouldn't stop."

Joseph looked like I'd struck him. He was clearly processing what I had told him, but he couldn't seem to wrap his head around it. "How did that turn into a lighter pointed at my balls?"

"You asked me what specialty I was declaring. When I told you that I wanted to work in the burn unit, you grabbed a lighter and threatened to set your dick on fire to see how good I would be at fixing it."

"What?" He started laughing, which turned into choking, and before I knew it, Joseph was punching his chest with his fist.

"You were really drunk. But you were still an ass."

"Are you lying right now?" he asked through his laughter, which in turn made me start laughing too.

"No. Why would I lie about this?"

"Because it's ridiculous. And as far as I know, I've never behaved like that before."

"Like I said, you were really drunk."

"All this time, I thought you'd threatened to light my dick on fire for no reason."

I nodded. "Yeah, that sounds sane."

"That's my whole point!" he shouted before slamming a fist on the table.

He flipped his palm over and wagged his fingers at me, wanting me to put my hand in his. I did as he'd asked.

"I'm sorry. I'm so sorry I said those things to you. There's no excuse for it. And I have no idea why I would ever act like that to you. I didn't mean it."

"I know that now," I said because I did.

Joseph didn't look at me like I was unworthy of being a surgeon or like I should spend my time being a doting wife for some dickhole. He looked at me with pride in his eyes. And I liked it. Way, way, way too much.

MUST BE THE VODKA

JOSEPH

WHAT AN ABSOLUTE fucking asshole I'd been to this woman from the moment I'd met her. I wanted to defend my actions in my head, but I couldn't even do that. There was no excuse. I'd never degraded someone I didn't know before, and I had no idea why I'd chosen Sutton, of all people, to do that to.

No wonder she'd always hated me. She had every right. I would have hated me too. It was a wonder how Kayla had even gotten her to agree to do this for me in the first place. Knowing what I knew now, I thought it was a fucking miracle that I was sitting across from her.

Oh, right. The money. I almost forgot about the money.

"You never told Kayla what happened that night between us," I said as I remembered that Kayla had told me she didn't know what had been said, only that we had been fighting.

"No. I was too embarrassed."

Our server set down a plethora of appetizers and small plates between us before asking if we'd like another round. I nodded, and she left. I'd asked for one of everything because I wasn't sure what Sutton was in the mood for, but I knew that she needed to eat something.

"Eat," I demanded before asking, "And why were you embarrassed to tell Kayla? I should have been the one who was embarrassed here."

Sutton picked up a fork and pulled the plate of Brussels sprouts toward her. "The whole thing was embarrassing. And I think your words struck a nerve. I'd never really felt beautiful, and when you said I should be a trophy wife, I couldn't help but think of how wrong you were. How no one would ever consider me that. Not with all the scars."

"Stop," I said. "Your scars don't define you. And I'd kiss every fucking one until you got that through your head if you let me."

"Joseph," she moaned as she looked away from me.

"Don't say things like that if you don't mean them. I can't take it. Not from you."

"What does that mean?"

"It means …" she started to say but stopped.

I knew she was fighting an internal battle with words I was dying to hear, so I pressed and pushed and begged to get her to say it all out loud.

"It means that I know this is supposed to be fake, but my feelings aren't. They're real, and they are growing a little more for you all the time."

"Because of the money?" I asked, knowing it was a shit thing to say but I couldn't seem to help myself. I was like some sort of self-sabotaging asshole who didn't know how to accept love.

She looked so damn offended, but honestly, it was a fair question.

Wasn't it?

"I keep forgetting about the money," she said quietly as she forked one of the sprouts and put it in her mouth.

"Me too," I admitted before feeling like a fucking idiot. That was something I couldn't allow myself to forget about. That was how I'd get taken advantage of—by letting my heart take precedence over my head.

Sutton sucked in a long breath as our next round of drinks arrived. “I’m not sure I can drink another.”

She laughed, but I slid it closer to her.

“You deserve it after the night you’ve had.”

“Me? Your mom is probably going to disown you, and now, she’s never going to leave the country or the company. You’ll be stuck with her forever. We failed.” She grabbed the drink she had just claimed she couldn’t have and swirled the straw around before taking a sip.

“I thought we talked about that already. My mother will be fine. We didn’t fail. We stick to the plan.”

“Right!” Sutton pointed at me with the straw before putting it back in the drink. “Stick to the plan.” She took another swig before looking at me, her green eyes all doe-like and sincere, like I could take her to my bed and have my fucking way with her if I asked.

“I should probably get you home,” I suggested, and she looked crestfallen before she pulled her expression together and forced a grin.

“Oh, okay,” she agreed like I had known she would.

Tonight’s food and drinks would go on my credit card

that the speakeasy had on file, so there was nothing to handle or deal with before leaving. Sutton moved toward the way we had come in, but I reached for her shoulders and spun her in the other direction.

"The exit's over there." I pointed toward a dimly lit doorway in the corner.

"This place is weird," she said before clearing her throat and adding, "but in an awesome way. I've never been anywhere like it."

"Privacy, remember?"

"I remember."

I'd already fired off a text message to my driver, letting him know where to get us, so when we exited into the freezing air, I wasn't surprised to see him waiting for us, rear door open and the car running. Sutton started to bend down to get into the car when I stopped her.

"Sutton, wait," I said, and she turned to face me. There were no other thoughts in my head, except wanting to claim this woman as mine. I grabbed the back of her neck and pulled her mouth toward me.

The second my lips pressed against hers, I was a goner. Her mouth opened, and my tongue moved inside as my fingers fisted in her hair, holding her close. I was possessed. And possessive. And I never wanted to stop. But when clapping started from somewhere in the distance, I blinked and pulled away. It was a harsh reminder that we were on a public street even if the people cheering were doing it from a distance.

"Sorry," I immediately apologized, but Sutton was grinning.

"I'm not," she said.

I wanted to strip her naked and fuck her in the backseat until she lost her voice from screaming my name, but I stopped myself.

"Time to get you home," I said before doing exactly that, fighting my desires the entire time.

I'D CROSSED A line last night. Eventually, it would have been crossed anyway, but it would have been done because it was part of the deal, a perk of the arrangement. Last night had had nothing to do with either of those things and everything to do with my inability to keep my dick in my pants, so to speak.

When Mother walked into my office and closed the door behind her, I wanted to throw punches. I wasn't in the mood to be lectured, and I knew that was what I was in for.

"What is it, Mother?" I asked, my tone snarky and rude.

"Don't take that tone with me. And you know damn well why I'm here," she said, her head shaking in disapproval.

"Spit it out then."

"That poor girl. Do you know what you've done to her? I meant what I said last night, Joseph. Have you even thought this through? What bringing her to Social Month will do to her life? It will be in complete upheaval. It will be invaded. She will no longer have privacy of any kind. Ever. Please tell me you at least thought about that before I brought it up."

She made an irritated sound, followed by the clucking of her tongue. "No, you couldn't have. Because if you had, you wouldn't be in this predicament."

"Stop!" I shouted. "Just stop for one second. Listen to yourself."

"It's you who needs to listen to me. Did you even see the pictures this morning?"

This was news to me and got me to take a breath.

"What pictures?" I pulled up a search engine and started frantically typing my name in an image search.

"They're grainy, but it's you. In some alleyway. Kissing your new"—she shrugged her shoulders—"whatever she is."

The pictures immediately flooded my desktop screen. They weren't clear, like Mother had said, but you could definitely tell that it was me. And since we'd already made a public outing the other night, you could tell it was Sutton as well.

I put a hand up. "Okay, hold on a second," I said before gathering my thoughts. "You were the one who was going to set me up with random strangers in the first place if I didn't bring a date to Social Month, remember?"

"Yes, and your point?"

"You didn't care about the press destroying those women's lives? You only care about them messing with Sutton's? Why is that? Do you not think she's good enough for me or something?" I felt myself getting extremely defensive. If my mom was about to tell me that I shouldn't be with Sutton, I was going to lose it.

"Whomever I planned on setting you up with already lives in the public eye. The press would be nothing new to her. She is equipped to handle what being seen with you would mean. Sutton has no idea. She isn't ready. Have you checked in on her this morning? They basically printed her biography in the *Post*."

I slammed my fist on top of my desk in anger. I felt out of control and like I was failing Sutton somehow by not protecting her the way I'd promised her I would.

"Calm down, Joseph," my mother warned as she moved toward the door and pulled it open. She knew that doing that would ensure that Kayla overheard what she said next.

"I suggest you stop this charade and give Sutton some semblance of peace. They'll leave her alone if you end things now. There's still time to save her from the fire you've thrown her in." She turned her back to me but continued talking loud enough for me to hear. "I'm sure you agree, don't you, Kayla?"

I wanted to rip my fucking hair out, but Kayla came in

and filled the space my mother had just left behind.

"Did you see what the *Post* wrote?" Her eyes were glossy, and I wondered if she'd been crying.

"No. What happened?" I pushed out from my desk and stalked toward my assistant.

"They posted about her scars. They found out about her being burned," Kayla said, her head shaking like she was disgusted.

"How?" I asked before realizing that this was exactly what my mother was talking about.

The press loved to dig up the past, and they'd stop at nothing until they found a topic so sensational that they could profit off of it or at least get more views.

"I don't know. This is all my fault," she said before sitting down on my couch and putting her face in her hands.

"This isn't your fault. It's mine."

She looked up at me, disappointment and pain written all over her face. "But I set you two up. I suggested that you date her, and I pushed her into it. I wouldn't let her say no. I didn't even think about this part."

Neither had I, but I didn't want to admit to being so

naive and stupid to Kayla. I was typically smarter than this, had all my ducks in a row and wasn't easily fooled.

"Is Sutton okay? Do you know? Have you talked to her?"

"Only for a second this morning. I don't think she's in a good place," she said.

I started grinding my teeth, wanting to destroy each and every person who'd had a hand in hurting her.

"Push my meetings," I bit out. "I need to make sure she's all right."

"You actually care about her," Kayla said as if the realization had just hit her.

"I do," I admitted before grabbing my keys and leaving the office, thankful that I'd decided to drive into work this morning instead of arranging for a car.

END THE CHARADE

SUTTON

WHAT HAD GONE from the hottest kiss in my entire life had quickly soured overnight. The freaking *Post* had somehow found out about my burns and written about them. It was mortifying. The most private thing in my life was now splashed across the internet for strangers to read and judge me for. I was thankful that there hadn't been any photographs accompanying the article, but their word choices were dramatic enough to paint a pretty descriptive picture.

It was one thing for me to have feelings and opinions about my scars, but it was another for someone who had never even seen them to describe them as "traumatizing" and "unflattering." I truly hadn't been prepared for this level of invasion. Even after Joseph's mom had mentioned it last night, it hadn't occurred to me that the press would stoop this low. And for what reason? Who the hell cared to know this much about me?

ME?!

I wasn't mad at Joseph per se, but I was mad.

Everyone at work had at least seen the article, and while most didn't say anything out loud, they all stared when I passed by, no doubt wondering what my scars looked like. Eventually, I had to be pulled into Human Resources before being sent home for the day. They'd told me that my *personal life was disrupting the hospital* and they needed to figure out how to proceed.

The buzzer at the apartment alerted me that someone was at my front door, and I wondered who the heck would be at my house before noon. Standing up to answer the call, I was only a little surprised to hear Joseph's voice responding back to me.

I pressed the button that allowed him entrance into the building and walked over to the front door to unlock it before sitting down at our tiny kitchen table. Joseph stormed through the door, almost breaking it off the hinges, his blue eyes searching the room until landing on me.

"Sutton, I'm so sorry. Are you okay?" He knelt in front of my body and wrapped his strong arms around me.

I pushed him off, so I could look at him. "Not really. How'd you know I was here?"

"I went to the hospital first. They told me you went home."

Putting up a finger, I stopped him. "They sent me home. I didn't come home voluntarily. They made me leave," I said, starting to get choked up. If I lost my job because of this fake arrangement bullshit, I'd never forgive him.

Joseph pushed himself upright and sat in the other chair at the table. "They sent you home? What reason did they give?"

He switched into business mode quicker than I'd taken a breath.

"Something about my personal life being a distraction."

"How long did they ask you to stay away?"

"Just today. That's all they said. Oh my gosh, can they tell me to never come back? To take a leave?"

"You've done nothing wrong. And you don't have to go anywhere even if they ask you to. There are protocols in place for things like this. We live in New York, for fuck's sake. I'm sure you've had celebrities or high-profile clients in your hospital before," he said.

I wasn't sure if he was asking me a question or not, but I answered him anyway. "We have. Numerous times."

"Then, they know how to handle publicity. They just weren't prepared for it coming from within."

"Can they fire me?"

"Not legally. And I'll sue the hell out of them if they try."

I know Joseph meant every word. He would sue them and do everything in his power to win. But I'd still be jobless and have to start over somewhere new. Most likely, I'd be blackballed by every other hospital in the city, and then what? I'd have to move out of state in order to work? I loved living in New York. I loved working at my hospital. At least I had up until this morning's awkwardness.

"I don't think I can do this. It's too much. Your mom was right." I couldn't look at him while I said the words. I was afraid to see his expression.

"You're breaking up with me?" His voice broke, and it took a piece of me with it.

"How can we break up when we were never together in the first place?"

"No."

"No what?" I asked, finally focusing on him.

He was staring right at me, his eyes intent, his features steeled and strong.

"No. I'm not letting you break up with me or whatever it is you think you're doing."

I scoffed, irritated and turned on at his brashness. "Oh, you're not *letting* me?"

"Listen to me, Sutton. You'll tell me to leave, and I'll go but only because you asked and not because I wanted to," he pointed out before continuing, his tone almost bored, "and then we'll both be sad, pretending like we made the right decision, but we'll both secretly know that we didn't. I'll miss you but be way too arrogant to ever tell you. Your life will be unbearable without me in it, but you'll be too embarrassed to admit it. And then Kayla will have to intervene and get us back together, where we always belonged in the first place."

I laughed out loud, but I could clearly picture the reality of what he'd just said. Or maybe it was one too many Hallmark movies as a kid that had me believing his diatribe. "That's a very intricate story."

"And it's true. I like you. I want to be with you, so I'm skipping all that in-between stuff I just mentioned and staying put by telling you, no, you're not breaking up with me."

He was insane. I mean, we still had so much to learn about one another. What if we weren't even compatible really? Sure, we had chemistry and attraction, but that wasn't what made a relationship stick.

"We barely know each other," I tried to argue, but he threw his chair back as he stood up and started pacing, his fingers running through his dark hair.

"That's bullshit, and you know it," he fired back at me as his pacing halted. "I know that you're smart. And fun. And brutally honest. And that even though I said horrible things to you the first time we met, you still put that shit aside in order to help me. You have a big heart. You're strong. Independent. And I know you don't need me. Not for one second do I think you need me, but I need you. I want you."

My eyes filled with moisture, and I didn't want to cry, but I couldn't stop it if I tried. I wiped at my eyes with the back of my hand, and just when I thought I couldn't take hearing another word out of his mouth, he gave me more.

"You're sexy as hell, and all I can think about is touching every inch of your body and worshipping it until you understand just how gorgeous I think you are. Inside and out."

"Did you practice that speech?" I asked as more tears fell.

He let out a gruff laugh. "No. That was straight from the heart."

Before I knew it, he was kneeling in front of me again, his blue eyes watching me, his hands touching me, his voice preparing me. "I'm going to kiss you now."

And he did. Jesus, he kissed me slow, his tongue moving like he had all the time in the world. His arms wrapped around me as he lifted me out of the chair and into his arms, our mouths still fused together as he walked down my narrow hallway.

"Which door?"

"Last on the left," I said, and he was kissing me again.

The feel of his tongue and the warmth of his lips lit my whole body on fire. Every nerve ending exploded at once, and I knew I'd never felt anything this intense before.

He placed me on top of my bed before hovering over me, his eyes roving over every inch of me from my head to my toe. It was a little unnerving, but I sucked in a breath and tried to feel as beautiful as he kept telling me I was.

But I couldn't get the article out of my head. That damn article.

"Did you read it?" I asked, and he shushed me, putting a finger against my lips to keep me quiet.

"Yes," he said. "I'll deal with them later. First, I want to take care of my girl."

"Your girl, huh?" I asked around the finger he still had there.

"I thought we'd established that in the kitchen. Are you confused?" He pulled his hand away and gave me an inquisitive look.

"No," I replied in a whisper. "I just like hearing it."

"Good. Then, tell me who I am." He leaned down to

kiss my mouth but stopped short, teasing me. " 'Cause I'd like to hear it too."

"My man?" I said, but it came out sounding like a question more than anything else.

"Say it like you mean it."

"You're mine. My man."

"Damn straight."

He raised his eyebrows before claiming my lips once more, and I groaned into his mouth, feeling safe and secure in his arms. I felt like I'd stepped into some sexual fairy tale, where everything Joseph did and said sent shock waves of pleasure through my body. He almost made me forget about the scars.

Almost.

"I'm going to take off your top now, okay?"

It was sweet, the way he asked first before doing it, like he could read my mind. He knew there was no way in the world I was going to tell him no, but he still waited for me to tell him yes before actually going through with it.

"Okay," I said.

He reached the hem, lifting the shirt up and over my head before tossing it to the side. He sucked in a breath, and I instantly dreaded what that sound meant, thinking he didn't like what he saw.

"No, Sutton," he said, leaning down to kiss my exposed stomach, his lips touching the place where my scars first started. Or maybe it was where they ended. "You're so damn beautiful. And I won't pretend that the scars aren't there. But I also won't pretend like they're all I see when I look at you," he explained.

My hands moved through his hair as he continued to run his tongue around the puckered flesh, pressing kisses to all the parts I'd once believed were too disfigured to love.

"Thank you."

He lifted his head to make eye contact, the question written all over his face.

"For talking about them. For not acting like they don't exist."

I'd never known that I needed that—for them to be acknowledged instead of ignored. For him to touch them, kiss them, and not be repulsed by them.

He crawled back up my body. He kissed my mouth and then worked his way lower. His lips grazed my neck, my collarbone, and once he unclasped my bra and threw it off, he gave each breast equal attention. My back arched in response to his tongue playing with my nipple as his fingers worked their way lower, unfastening my jeans and attempting to get them off. I lifted my hips, helping him without saying a word as he tugged them off like his life depended on it.

Before I knew it, I was lying there, completely exposed in only a thong. "I'm basically naked, and you're still fully clothed."

He looked down at his body, stopped touching me, and said, "You're right," before leaning back and pushing off the bed.

I watched him stand, reach for his shirt, and unbutton it one at a time before dropping it to the floor. It was the first time I'd seen him with no shirt on in real life.

"This is much better than the pictures Kayla taped up in the hallway," I said, and he shot me an inquisitive look.

"There were pictures?" he asked as he started working on his slacks, slow and torturous, as if he knew exactly what he was doing.

"Lots of pictures. But like I said, this is better." I

waved an arm up and down the length of his gorgeous, sculpted body.

His hardness stood out from his boxers, and I couldn't stop staring at it.

"Are you looking at my junk?" he said, and the term made me giggle.

"Just remembering how you almost burned it off, is all," I said, and he grinned before hopping back on the bed, straddling my body.

"I'm going to make you very happy that I didn't." He pulled down my panties with his teeth before pulling his boxers off as well.

"I can see that," I commented as I reached down with my hand and held it, slowly stroking up and down.

"Sutton, you have to stop." His voice sounded strained.

"Only if you put that perfect penis inside me," I demanded as I continued stroking. "That's the only way to stop me."

"Sutton," he groaned, "I didn't bring a condom. I came from the office. I didn't plan on this."

"I have one." I maneuvered underneath the weight of his body, reached for the nightstand, and slid it open, fiddling around inside. “Ha! Here!”

“I don’t want to know why you have a nightstand full of condoms, do I?” He took the square package out of my hand and ripped the corner open with his teeth.

“I’m a doctor,” I said. “Safety first.”

“Uh-huh.” He pulled it from the wrapper and positioned it at the tip before rolling it down the length.

“I’m ready. I want this. I want you.”

He cut my words off with a kiss, his mouth claiming mine, his tongue sweeping in and sharing my air as he pushed his dick toward my entrance and inside. I sucked in a harsh breath, my hands wrapping around his neck.

I couldn’t get enough of the feel of his skin against mine. The sharpness of his freshly shaven scruff, rough against my cheek. His hard muscles pressing into my body. His fingertips gripping me so hard that I knew they’d leave bruises later.

He worked in and out of my body, his penis filling me in the best possible way.

“I’m so glad,” I said between labored breaths, “that you didn’t light your pants on fire that night.”

“You and me both,” he said before fucking me harder and holding me tighter until we both came.

HANDLING MY BUSINESS

JOSEPH

THE HIGH OF an orgasm was almost unexplainable. There were no words that gave it justice, that properly conveyed the way coming inside a woman truly felt. But coming down from that high was a different story altogether. Everything sank in all at once—the reality of what you'd just done, who you'd done it with, what it meant, and how it might change things.

Lying next to Sutton, holding her in my arms, I couldn't imagine feeling happier or more content as my fingers drew lazy circles on her shoulder.

"Are you okay?" I asked because even though I felt amazing, I refused to assume that she felt the same.

She lifted her head from my chest and peered at me through hazy green eyes. "Of course. Are you?"

"Never better," I said, pressing a kiss to her head. "Except I need to get back to the office. Kayla's going to kill me."

Sutton let out a laugh. "You're probably right. I mean, it is still daytime, and you've been here awhile."

"I don't want to, but I need to go," I said as my stomach muscles contracted.

I moved to sit up, and Sutton pushed away from me, pulling a sheet up against her chest.

"I know. It's okay," she reassured me. "Unless you're never going to talk to me again. Then, I might choose some other words to say."

"You think I'm going to ghost you?" I asked, referring to when someone disappeared and never talked to the other person again. "Not a chance. You're stuck with me."

"Then, I'm not upset." She smiled, and I tucked an errant strand of red hair behind her ear. "Go. Thank you for the orgasm. Come again soon."

This woman was incredible. Just when I thought I couldn't be more into her, she said shit like that. I gave her a kiss on the cheek, and then I got out of bed and gathering my pants before stepping into them.

"Sutton, I need to ask you some things."

"Okay." She had no idea what I was about to say.

"It's about the article." I watched her expression carefully, measuring it.

She didn't look particularly fazed or upset by what I had said, more genuinely curious about where I was going with the topic.

"The one in the *Post*," she clarified.

I nodded as I started buttoning my shirt, which was now wrinkled to hell. Thankfully, I had a jacket in the car, so hopefully, no one would notice my unprofessional attire.

"Yeah. Was it exaggerated or sensationalized in any way? They tend to do that, and I need to know."

Her eyes pulled together. She was still clearly confused about my line of questioning. This woman had no idea that I needed all of the facts before I went to the *Post* and took care of this.

"I know they do, but no, it really wasn't. They didn't say anything that was untrue." She shrugged a shoulder, the sheets still wrapped firmly around her chest as she watched my every move. "It was honestly just more embarrassing than anything else. To have that personal information printed for everyone to see without my consent or knowledge."

Pressing my lips together, I practically had to bite my cheek to stop myself from saying all the things I wanted to say. "I understand completely. And I'm very sorry this happened, but it won't happen again."

"You can't say that, Joseph. You don't own the press," she said.

I bit back a laugh because money had bought me lots of things in the past, the press included.

"I'll call you after work," I said as I bent down to give her a kiss good-bye. "I can see my way out, but please lock the door behind me."

"Maybe I'll leave it wide open," she teased, knowing that her response would torment me.

"Don't make me hire security to stand outside your door, Sutton. I will," I threatened, but it wasn't an empty threat, and we both knew it.

"Go to work!" she yelled.

And I left her and my heart in her apartment.

"CALL KAYLA," I said as I started my car, and the phone rang through the speakers.

"I swear to God, you'd better be on your way back here," Kayla said when she answered.

"I am, but I need to make two detours first," I said, and she groaned.

"You are making my job very difficult. You know how much I hate rescheduling meetings and calls, especially when they're overseas."

"I know, but this is important. Tell them that a personal emergency came up. They'll be pissed, but they'll understand. I've never used that as an excuse before," I instructed as I checked my mirrors and put on my turn signal.

"What are you doing, boss? At least tell me, so I can either be pissed or impressed," she said as I pulled out into traffic, annoyed at how crowded the streets were in the middle of the afternoon.

What the hell were all these people doing, driving around?

"I'm going to the *Post* and then to Sutton's work."

Kayla exhaled loudly into the phone, and it made a horrible noise throughout my car. “Impressed it is,” she finally said.

“Since I’ll be in the car for a few, why don’t you try to get London back on the line, and I’ll talk to them now?”

It worked out perfectly. My conversation with my contacts in London ended right as I pulled into the *Post*’s parking structure. Cutting the engine, I exited the car and straightened my suit before walking inside the building with basically no plan.

I was met with security as soon as I entered.

“Can I help you?”

“I need to see Daisy Darling,” I said, almost snickering at the clearly made-up name.

“Is she expecting you?” he asked as he scanned a clipboard filled with printed-out pages.

“She is not.”

Before I could add anything else to my response, he pointed me toward a desk where a lone female sat behind a computer.

I walked over.

“Hi there. How can I help you?”

"I need to see Daisy Darling," I repeated the request. "She is not expecting me, but she will want to see me. Please tell her that Joseph Martin would like to speak with her."

As soon as my name left my lips, the woman straightened her back and turned uncomfortable. "Of course. One second while I ring her line," she said, clearing her throat.

I tapped my fingers on the desk and waited.

"She'll see you. Take the elevator up to floor seven." She waved a hand in the direction of a bank of elevators before handing me a sticky paper. "Here's your guest pass. Please make sure you wear it someplace visible at all times."

Placing the sticker over my chest, I thanked her and made my way to the elevators, passing the security guard on my way. When I arrived on the seventh floor, I had no idea what to expect. I'd never given the *Post* much thought, couldn't have cared less when they printed lies about me or used my name to sell papers. But this—bringing Sutton into things—was unacceptable.

"Mr. Martin," a tall brunette woman greeted me as

soon as I stepped out. "I'm surprised to see you here." She gave me a flirtatious grin. "Kind of."

"I take it, you're Miss Darling?" I said the name like it tasted as ridiculous as it sounded.

"I am."

"Do you have somewhere we can speak privately?" I made sure that my tone wasn't threatening. I wanted her to feel comfortable, to believe that I wasn't angry. I planned on saving my anger and threats for when we were alone.

"There's a conference room we can use," she said as she turned her back and navigated through a maze of cubicles.

My mere presence was enough to get tongues wagging and eyes bulging. It seemed like everyone stopped what they were doing to watch my every move.

Daisy paused in front of an oversize mahogany door and held it with one arm. "Here," she said.

As I stepped inside the room, I was thankful that no one else was waiting for us. It'd occurred to me for a split second that I might be walking into some sort of press ambush I wasn't prepared for. I really hadn't thought this through.

She closed the door behind us and sat across from the seat I'd chosen at the table. "How can I help you?"

"It was pretty fucked up, what you printed today." I jumped right in, and she leaned forward, that stupid grin still on her face.

"And why's that? What was so fucked up about it?" she asked, clearly assuming that she had the upper hand.

"Do you get off on writing about other people's pain? Does exploiting an accident to sell papers make you feel good? Really warm your heart?"

"First of all, it's my job to write things that make money. But in case you didn't actually read the article—" she started, and I cut her off.

"I read it. I read every word."

"Then, you know that I didn't write a single lie. I wrote the truth. They just happened to be things that no one else knew yet."

She looked impressed with herself. Like she deserved some kind of award for *not* exaggerating or sensationalizing Sutton's situation.

"Those are things that no one has a right to know." I was getting pissed again. That uncontrollable anger I felt when things were out of my control and I knew it.

Daisy cleared her throat and threw her head back. "The public has a very personal interest in you. You sell a lot of papers. You get a lot of hits online. She is now a part of you, so yes, they might not have a *right* to know those things, but they *want* to know them."

I snapped my mouth shut and breathed in and out through my nose. I wanted to threaten her, to tell her not to ever write about Sutton again or she wouldn't like the outcome of her actions. But I knew that I couldn't do that. Anything I said in here could be used against me. She'd write about it the second I left this office.

"Why did you come here today?" she asked, breaking me from my thoughts.

"I don't want you to write about her scars again. It's rude. It's mean. It's a shitty thing to do. She doesn't deserve the public knowing that kind of stuff about her."

I watched as the sly grin faded and her expression turned.

"I have pictures," she said. "After the article came out, I got an anonymous email that had pictures attached."

"How do you know it's Sutton?"

"Her face is in them."

"What do you want?" I asked, and she looked confused for only a second. "To not print them. Ever. What do you want?"

Daisy sat silent for a moment, measuring me with her eyes that had on way too much makeup. She looked like she was ready for a night out, not a workday.

"Exclusives," she said simply, and I nodded.

"I'll give you pictures of us before we even arrive at any of the Social Month events. I'll get you behind-the-scenes photos. Us getting ready. In our homes. Things like that," I offered as I pulled out my phone and started typing up a quick email to Kayla. I needed her to get something ready for me and send it over as soon as possible.

"Yeah"—she nodded, her face lighting up—"I like that. I also want one other thing."

"What?" I finished typing, pressed Send, and waited.

"An exclusive joint interview with you both as a couple. Your first before anyone else."

"Done."

"How do you know I won't print the pictures anyway?"

"Because before I leave this office, you're going to sign a document that says you won't. And if you do, I'll sue you personally. Not the *Post.* You. And I'll make sure you never work in journalism again. Not even if you try to start a blog."

I planned on delivering the same exact message to the "anonymous" emailer of the photos as well. There was only one person who could have done it; Sutton's ex. He wouldn't even think about breathing her name after I finished with him.

Refreshing the email app on my phone, I watched as Kayla's response came up with a document attached. "I need a printer."

MY NEXT STOP took me to Sutton's work, where I was already vaguely familiar with the hallways and the layout. When I walked into the main lobby, the nurse from the other day recognized me immediately and rolled her eyes as I approached.

"You know she's not here. I told you that earlier."

"I know. Where's your HR office? Can you tell them I

need to speak with them? Urgently."

She made a sound of disapproval before picking up the phone and saying things I couldn't hear from behind the glass that separated us. "Fourth floor, make a right. They're expecting you."

When I exited the elevator this time, I was greeted by a man in a suit. "Mr. Martin," he said before extending his hand for me to shake. "Come with me."

I followed him into a room, down a long hallway, and into a private office, where he closed the door behind us.

"How can I help you?"

"I'm here on behalf of Sutton. She doesn't know I'm here," I clarified before I continued, "I know that her dating me has brought some challenges into the workplace."

He scoffed. "To say the least, Mr. Martin."

"That's not her fault. And I know for a fact that you have protocols in place to deal with things like this," I said, and he interrupted me.

"We do, but they're temporary. They aren't meant to last long-term. We have no idea how her dating you will affect this hospital on a day-to-day basis, but if the past couple of days are any indication, then we're not equipped."

"Monetarily?" I asked, knowing that they had room in the budget for unplanned events, but most likely not to handle something like this for months on end.

"Yes," he said before grimacing.

"And that's why I'm here. I'll cover the costs for extra security as long as you feel it's necessary. I want Sutton to be safe at work. As well as all of your employees. Will that be a problem?"

"I don't foresee it being one, but I need to run it by my superiors."

"Do that and get back to me by the end of the day." I pulled out a business card and handed it to him. "And one more thing. You can't punish Sutton for what's happening. This does not affect her work, her workload, or any of her training. Are we clear? No more forced days off."

"I understand. The extra security will help," he said before adding, "I'll be in touch."

I felt like I could finally breathe.

Hopefully, Sutton would feel the same when she found out about what I'd done and not be upset with me for doing it.

EPILOGUE

SUTTON

SIX MONTHS LATER

IF I HADN'T seen Joseph leave my apartment building in his car that afternoon, I would have sworn he rode off on a white horse, cape flying, sword raised.

He'd apparently gone straight to the *Post* to work out a deal on my behalf and then to my hospital to fix things there as well. It was more than I had ever expected and something I never would have asked him to do.

I didn't care what people called him in the press and online. They were wrong, and they didn't know him the way I did. He was a godsend. And he was mine.

When Social Month had finally rolled around, none of what we were doing in public had been an act anymore. Nothing about our relationship was fake, and to be honest, maybe it never had been. Looking back at it now, I thought that even when I'd hated him, there was something more lingering just behind the veil … something softer, something more along the lines of love and less like hate.

We posed for pictures, made out in front of throngs of people, held hands, and gazed into each other's eyes—the way people in love tended to do. Our photos were splashed across various media outlets, but only one—the *Post*—had pictures that no one else did. That was the deal Joseph had worked out with the reporter there.

And when the two of us met with her one snow-filled afternoon for our first joint interview ever, she actually apologized to me for writing the article about my burns and exposing the fact that I was badly scarred without giving me a heads-up or any kind of warning. We talked about what her report had done and how it had affected me emotionally and professionally. She put part of our conversation in her final article but not before sending it to me first for my approval. It was a kindness she hadn't had to offer but had, and I respected her for it. Joseph and I continued to work with Daisy exclusively, which gave her a little more credibility. And when she took a job at a more reputable company, we followed her there as well.

Everything between us fell into place so easily and quickly that no one around us questioned it. Not even when he paid off my student loans behind my back even though I'd told him not to. I figured his mom would think I was using him for his money, but she never once accused me of that or thought it. Trust me, I'd asked.

"I'm doing this for us," Joseph kept saying whenever I fought him on the subject until, one day, it finally clicked for me.

We weren't temporary.

What we had was real, and it was going to last forever. He hadn't paid off my loans to help clear my debt; he had done it for us, for our future, because there would be an us until the day we died.

And when he slipped that massive diamond ring on my finger one night during dessert, hiding it inside of some elaborate chocolate horse-and-carriage design, I started crying. When Kayla, his mom, and my parents suddenly appeared out of nowhere, I cried even harder. Joseph was always thinking of everything, leaving no stone unturned.

"Oh, sweetheart, he's such a catch," my mom

whispered in my ear as she gushed over my ring.

"I like him a lot," my dad added.

I hugged them both, so thankful that they were there for this moment.

"I really can leave now," his mom said, her own tears spilling down her cheeks. "But don't you dare get married until I get back!"

"But you won't be back for a year," Joseph complained, but I rested a hand on his shoulder, instantly calming him.

"We can wait," I said, reassuring him that there was no rush. "We need at least a year to plan it anyway," I added, and he didn't seem to understand why.

"All the good venues are booked a year out," Kayla added, and Joseph looked perplexed.

I didn't want to think about any of that stuff right now. I wanted to enjoy being engaged to the man of my dreams, who had tried to burn his dick off the night we first met.

"I can't believe you're going to marry my boss," Kayla whispered as she wrapped an arm around my shoulders and gave me a tight squeeze. "Does that make you my boss-in-law?"

A loud laugh escaped me. "It's all your fault. You're the one who set us up."

"I know. I deserve a raise."

"He just gave you a raise."

"I want another one. You're moving out soon," she whined, her bottom lip jutting out in a pout.

I'd already started packing my stuff, slowly bringing boxes over to Joseph's place so that it happened gradually instead of overnight.

"Future wife," Joseph said as he kissed my lips.

"Future husband," I responded, the words making chills race down my spine.

"I can't wait to make you my wife. Let's go get married right now," he suggested, and I laughed again.

"No," I argued, but I wasn't sure why.

"Whatever. Your parents love me, by the way," he said, giving a nod toward where my parents stood, talking his mom's ear off.

"It's only fair since your mom loves me."

And she did. I had been worried at first that she wouldn't approve, but I couldn't have been more wrong. We got along better than I ever could have anticipated. She had only been so harsh that night in her penthouse because she had anticipated that I'd be overwhelmed and upset by bad press—like what had happened with the *Post* article—and she was genuinely worried She didn't think I could handle the pressure and stress that went along with dating someone in the public eye.

She'd told me one day that she had never been more grateful to be wrong. "You're the perfect person for my son."

I'd cried again.

I was always freaking crying, it seemed.

My parents went back to Boston, and Joseph's mom got ready to leave for her trip, signing paperwork and notarizing things to make Joseph's role in the company official.

And when we dropped her off at the airport, where she boarded a private jet, I asked out loud, "How do you pack for something like that?"

She only had one suitcase and one carry-on bag. One of each!

"Knowing her, I'm sure she'll just buy everything she needs when she gets there," Joseph said, his arm wrapped around me as his mom got on board after telling us goodbye.

"How do you feel? Are you okay?" I looked at him, wondering if he felt abandoned, or free, or sad. Maybe it would hit him later that his mom wasn't around. I knew that it would be an adjustment of sorts.

"I'm not sure yet."

"Should we tell her I'm pregnant?" I asked, and he shushed me, his finger instantly over my lips.

"She'll never leave then. She's so excited to leave. Look at her," he said, and I went to argue but couldn't.

She looked so happy, so ready for her adventure that I didn't want to take that away from her.

Plus, we'd been disagreeing over how to handle this subject since the morning we'd found out I was expecting. It was all the crying. I couldn't stop anymore. A commercial with a kitten? I was bawling. A social media post about a military dad surprising his daughter at school? I was bawling. A deer befriending a puppy? You guessed it—bawling.

"She is never going to forgive us," I said, referring to us keeping the news from her, not the news itself. His mom was going to be over-the-moon excited about a baby.

"She will. We just need to tell her in a few months—after you've passed the first trimester and we have a due date. That way, she can decide if she wants to be here for the birth of her first grandchild or not."

I looked at him and stomped my foot. "Of course she'll want to be here!"

He kissed the side of my head. "I know. That's why we wait. So she can live a little first before coming back here."

"Fine, but when we finally do tell her, you'd better let her know it was your idea to make her wait, not mine."

"Deal," he said with a grin as the stairs started folding up into the plane and his mom waved at us from her seat at the window.

We both enthusiastically waved back, like we were the ones going away and not her. The plane started to pull away, maneuvering toward the runway in the distance, and I stood there in Joseph's arms, leaning against him, feeling safe and at peace.

"I can't believe you let me put a baby in you," he said against my head, my hair sticking to his lips before he brushed it away.

We still weren't sure what had happened or *how* we had gotten pregnant in the first place. I mean, of course we knew how it'd happened, but we had been safe every time we had sex—always using condoms, even when we didn't want to. One of them must have torn or had a hole in it or something. There was no other explanation for how I'd ended up this way.

"I can't believe you wanted to burn off your baby-maker to see if I could fix it," I said with a laugh, and he groaned.

"You're never going to let me live that down, are you?"

"Never," I added with a smile.

I was pretty sure I'd never stop smiling as long as this man was by my side. He was going to be an incredible father. An unbelievable dad.

And I was the lucky woman who got to make him one. All because of a fake arrangement that had turned into something more. Way more.

Thank you so much for reading! I hope you enjoyed Sutton & Joseph's story as much as I did! It was a lot of fun to write and hopefully a lot of fun for you to read as well!

I came up with the idea for this series to give you all lighthearted & happy reads. But mostly, I just wanted you to enjoy yourself and get lost in a fictional world for a little while. I hope this story did that for you. And I hope all the rest will too!

Did you miss the very first one in the series—KISSING MY COWORKER? It's a workplace New Year's romance you won't want to miss!

Other Books by J. Sterling

Bitter Rivals—an enemies-to-lovers romance

Dear Heart, I Hate You

In Dreams—a new adult college romance

Chance Encounters—a coming-of-age story

THE GAME SERIES

The Perfect Game—Book One

The Game Changer—Book Two

The Sweetest Game—Book Three

The Other Game (Dean Carter)—Book Four

THE PLAYBOY SERIAL

Avoiding the Playboy—Episode #1

Resisting the Playboy—Episode #2

Wanting the Playboy—Episode #3

THE CELEBRITY SERIES

Seeing Stars—Madison & Walker

Breaking Stars—Paige & Tatum

Losing Stars—Quinn & Ryson

THE FISHER BROTHERS SERIES

No Bad Days—a new adult, second-chance romance

Guy Hater—an emotional love story

Adios Pantalones—a single-mom romance

Happy Ending

THE BOYS OF BASEBALL

(THE NEXT GENERATION OF FULLTON STATE BASEBALL PLAYERS):

The Ninth Inning—Cole Anders

Behind the Plate—Chance Carter

Safe at First—Mac Davies

FUN FOR THE HOLIDAYS

(A COLLECTION OF STAND-ALONE NOVELS WITH HOLIDAY-BASED THEMES)

Kissing My Coworker

Dumped for Valentine's

My Week with the Prince

Spring's Second Chance

Summer Lovin'

Falling for the Boss

About the Author

Jenn Sterling is a Southern California native who loves writing stories from the heart. Every story she tells has pieces of her truth in it as well as her life experience. She has her bachelor's degree in radio/TV/film and has worked in the entertainment industry the majority of her life.

Jenn loves hearing from her readers and can be found online at:

Blog & Website:

www.j-sterling.com

Twitter:

www.twitter.com/AuthorJSterling

Facebook:

www.facebook.com/AuthorJSterling

Instagram:

@ AuthorJSterling

If you enjoyed this book, please consider writing a spoiler-free review on the site from which you purchased it. And thank you so much for helping me spread the word about my books and for allowing me to continue telling the stories I love to tell. I appreciate you so much. :)

Thank you for purchasing this book.

Made in the USA
Middletown, DE
02 March 2023